LOTTERY OF REVENGE

A PSYCHOLOGICAL THRILLER (BOOK 3)

NADIJA MUJAGIC

Edited by Jessica Ryn
Cover art by https://www.rockingbookcovers.com/

SHE'S BACK... AND SHE KNOWS YOUR SECRETS

LOTTERY OF REVENGE

A PSYCHOLOGICAL THRILLER

NADIJA MUJAGIC

PART ONE

CHAPTER 1

THE SMALL ROOM IS SWELTERING.

I don't know if it's the hot weather or my menopausal hot flashes, but sweat is forming on my forehead, and I'm dying of thirst. I puff my tank top to get some relief, but it makes little difference. The heat is distracting, but I force myself to focus on the task at hand.

A mild dizziness has me wobbling on my feet as I lean in to get a better look at the computer screen. We've been at it for half an hour, and I flinch every time I see the familiar face.

Jimmy.

"Go back, go back," I ask.

This is probably the fifth time I've asked. I can't get enough of it.

Andrew rewinds the video once again, so I can study every little movement, every light shedding on the space, every single sequence that led to the ultimate disaster.

What I'm seeing in the video is clear. The hotel's

parking lot is sparse with cars, but there it is, my car tucked in the corner, trying to hide from Jimmy's view. The street-light projects a dim glare on the car, but it's enough to see Jimmy's movements.

That son of a gun was able to find my car.

In the video footage, he parades with a bag of tools to my vehicle like he owns it, gets down on his back and slides underneath. I immediately recognize that bag. He'd had it for decades and carried it around him whenever friends or acquaintances asked him to help repair their car. He seemed so proud of it, like it was the most valuable posses-sion in his life.

As Jimmy tampers with the brakes of my car, his feet stick out from underneath, occasionally moving from side to side. A slight wind picks up and moves the branches around, as if someone is shaking the trees. I remember it had been pouring with rain the day before, and I'd been resting in my hotel room, hiding from Jimmy.

After several minutes, Jimmy reemerges from under-neath the car and walks away from it. I can clearly see his face; an eerie feeling, knowing he is dead.

Killed by my very own hands.

"He looks so confident here," I whisper.

I watch Jimmy walk across the lot, which I assume is to his car, holding his bag, and looking like he's just won the jackpot.

Andrew shoots a gaze at me and nods. "I know. I think I see a smile cracking on his face."

We let the footage roll to the end this time, without

rewinding it back to the beginning. I cross my arms and stare at the screen, pouting. I knew what he'd done already, but it still sends shockwaves through me to watch him arrange my death so willingly.

It's a huge relief that Andrew could unearth the footage. If it wasn't for him, I'd be rotting in jail. God bless him.

Just as I sigh and uncross my arms, ready to move on with my life, a sudden commotion on the video stops me in my tracks. I gasp as a familiar car circles the lot, moving toward the exit. My eyes widen as I place my hand on my mouth and yelp, "Oh my God."

Andrew looks at me with concern in his eyes. "What is it?"

I point my index finger at the screen and try to push words out of my mouth.

It's that familiar car I've come to appreciate whenever it sits in the garage of my new home in Hampton. The blue Mustang.

The one that belonged to my daughter, Lucy.

But maybe it's not right. There are so many blue Mustangs out there. This one doesn't necessarily belong to Lucy. I tell Andrew to rewind the footage once again, so we can see what's inside the car. Or better, *who* is inside the car? He does as I ask and pauses on the part where the front of the car can be seen clearly.

"That's it."

I lean forward and stare at the screen, my mouth agape. From this angle, I'm sure I can see the face of a young woman inside the car. The image is blurry, but there's no question it has to be her.

Lucy.

Sickness churns in my stomach, and I want to throw up, but instead I sit down next to Andrew and hold on to the arm of the chair to stop myself fainting.

Lucy had witnessed Jimmy tamper with my car brakes?

Lucy was there, watching him, maybe even plotting with him. Heat rushes to my face, and I'm sure this time it's not hot flashes. It's hot, raw anger. My daughter knew Jimmy wanted to kill me, yet said nothing about it to me.

Well played, Lucy. But I *will* get my dignity back. I *will* get the peace and closure I deserve.

And from now on, no one will mess with the new-and-improved Lynn.

Never again.

CHAPTER 2

I KEEP SHAKING, staring at the screen for several moments after Andrew has turned it off. Lucy knew all along. How could she have kept such a vile secret from me and then behave like I was in the wrong the whole time?

No wonder she's vanished from my life. For the whole five years I've spent in jail, she didn't contact me once. Not one letter, not a visit. Even an angry note to cuss me out or disown me would have been better than nothing.

Silence can really hurt.

"Do you want to lie down, Lynn?" Andrew asks.

Andrew is a sweetheart as well as being an incredible private investigator, and he's been a rock ever since I hired him when I was trying to keep tabs on Jimmy.

I'd hired Andrew to follow Jimmy around and find out if he had anything to do with the stalker who'd emerged shortly after I won the lottery. At the time, Andrew couldn't trace anything suspicious. In fact, I'd acted so paranoid that he thought it could all be in my head.

Right after our last meeting, Andrew had gone missing. His phone got disconnected, and I had no way of getting in touch with him. He was my last hope, but he disappeared without a trace.

Joy had flooded through me when I finally heard from Andrew when I first went to jail. Out of the blue, I was told I had a visitor, and, to my surprise, I'd found Andrew sitting at the telephone booth, smiling at me. My jaw dropped when I saw his handsome figure looking at me.

The sight of him gave me a sliver of hope that maybe I wouldn't rot in jail until I died. Maybe he could dig up some more evidence that I'd killed Jimmy in self-defense, and that he'd tampered with my car brakes. And sure enough, it happened. Andrew came through.

"Well, you're all over the news, young lady." Andrew had grinned, holding the receiver to his ear. "I couldn't help but pay you a visit."

He'd explained that he'd been going through some personal issues and had to disappear for a while, and that's why I couldn't get hold of him back then. Then he apologized. But I was happy to see him back. It felt like he believed me, had faith in me. Believed I was framed and should be freed.

It's a good feeling when you have at least one person in life you can trust. One person is all it takes to continue on.

We devised a plan to do some more investigative work. He went to the fancy hotel I was staying in to get away from Jimmy, giving him the exact dates. I will never find out how he pulled it off, but to my shock, the hotel let

Andrew view the surveillance footage for the timeframe, and sure enough, he located a footage of Jimmy doing his misdeed.

He's my new hero.

The footage of Jimmy messing with my car brakes got me out of the jail early, along with my good behavior. The second part was easier than I thought.

But it wasn't just Andrew who'd helped set me free. My lawyer, Nick, was instrumental in making the arguments and appealing my case to the court.

But never in a million years did I think Lucy would have witnessed it and been quiet about it.

I nod and tell Andrew I want to lie down. I'm still so dizzy. I feel as if I'm living in a nightmare again, struggling to catch my breath.

Andrew leaves the room and comes back with a wet cloth and puts it gently on my forehead. In the other hand, he's holding a glass of iced water. "Here. Drink this."

I prop myself up and do as he asks. The cold water does wonders, despite this strange feeling in the pit of my stomach.

My daughter isn't who I thought she was. I can't believe I let her into my life so easily. But then—why wouldn't I? First, I was happy my child, the loss of whom I'd grieved for decades, was still alive. And second, she's my flesh and blood, the one who grew in my belly. How could I not accept her into my life? How could I not give our lives together a chance?

I knew it was all a mistake. And now I have evidence.

As I lie on the couch with my eyes closed, my mind churns with ideas.

I look at Andrew, who's spinning in the chair, watching me.

"Hey, Andrew," I say. "Do you know if the police knew about the footage?"

I wonder if the Hampton police did anything to cover up the evidence of Jimmy's intent to kill me. The police department has denied the accusations, of course, but I know they were eager to send me to jail. Even James, the retired cop who kept coming to my new house, had showed up at court and seemed thrilled I was going to serve a sentence. I saw that smirk on his face. The entire police department had been friends with Jimmy, thanks to his notorious ability to charm himself out of problems by fixing cops' cars for free and such. Jimmy was a crafty crook.

Andrew shrugs. "I honestly have no idea. It's hard to tell. You never know with the cops."

I turn around and stare at the wall, my mind spinning. I understand if the cops wanted me in jail, but why my own daughter? Nothing makes sense anymore.

I must find Lucy and tell her what I think of her. Close this chapter of my life for good. Andrew will help, I'm sure.

He stands up and hovers above me, watching me with his creased forehead. "Hey, sweetie, are you okay?"

I nod. I love that Andrew has become a good friend. He might be my only friend right now, and definitely the only one I can trust, but I'll take it. Better than none. He has no reason to betray me or send me to death like those from my past.

Plus, I'm paying him for his services, even though he kept refusing at first. Andrew felt guilty for disappearing, convinced that had he been around, I may never have felt I had to kill Jimmy, and he wanted to repay me somehow. Andrew's a good guy.

I appreciated his offer of free labor, but I couldn't accept it. At some point, people weigh the favors they've done, and I don't want to owe anyone anything. I prefer a clean deal.

"Hey, you want to grab dinner somewhere? Get your mind off of this … stuff?"

He can clearly tell how shook up I am. I swing my legs from the couch and sit up. I manage a small smile, even though I'm feeling a whirlwind of emotions inside. "Thanks, but I'll pass. Rain check?"

"Sure," he says.

We say our goodbyes that evening with the understanding we will be in touch soon to make further plans.

On my way home, I stop by a grocery store and pick up a few things, like iced tea and a loaf of bread. I usually eat before seven to satisfy my hunger, but not today. Bread is there just in case.

It's been less than a week since I got released from jail. And let me tell you, it feels like I've been reborn.

And I don't mean a feel-good type of reborn. I'm having to learn all the social etiquette over again. When I was in a store, I almost walked out without paying, because when was the last time I really paid for something? Or, when people said hi to me, I turned my head away, because that's what I did in jail to keep myself out of trouble. I stayed in my lane and refused to interact with other inmates. Instead, I buried my head in books, a new hobby I'd picked up, and kept myself occupied reading.

But I imagine being reborn is better than being imprisoned. With time, I'll get used to social norms and what-not. I need to be gentle with myself and give myself time to heal. Mentally, physically, emotionally.

As I pull into the parking lot of my apartment building, I check left and right, ensuring I don't see any of my neighbors. Ever since I got out of jail, they'd stare at me in passing, probably wondering how I'd appeared out of thin air. When I see them, I turn my head in the opposite direction, as I don't want to talk to them. It's because I'm hoping this living situation is temporary.

According to Andrew, someone has been living in my mansion, and I need to find out how they got in.

All fingers point to Lucy, as I'd given her access before going into jail, assuming I'd never get out, but Andrew had mentioned that a whole family had been seen going in and out. I will only be sure if she's involved when I get there. Either way, I will need to reclaim my home.

Then I can resume the calm, happy life I was always meant to live.

CHAPTER 3

THANKFULLY, HAVING ACCRUED FIVE YEARS' interest on my savings, my account is healthy, and I can still afford to rent a place outside my currently occupied mansion home.

I've rented an apartment just on the outskirts of Hampton, and I've purposely chosen one with ocean views and an easy ride to the beach. It's a two-bedroom apartment, on the top floor, fully furnished, at a whopping $3,000 a month. It's not cheap for New Hampshire standards, but I've decided to splurge after spending years in a five-by-five room overridden by the smell of urine and feces. I deserve that much.

When Lucy first entered my life, I'd worked hard to prove I was worthy of her love, respect, and trust. I put her down on the house deed and left it for her in my will. I wanted to make sure she was all set once I died, so she wouldn't need to worry about her future. I couldn't make up for all the love I couldn't give her all those decades, so this was the least I could do.

But after spending three years in prison, and with Lucy not visiting me once, I'd changed the deed and my will to remove Lucy's name. Instead, when I die, all the proceeds of my real estate would go to a charitable cause. To someone more deserving. At that point, I could only surmise Lucy wanted nothing to do with me, including my inheritance.

But of course, now I know she'd witnessed Jimmy sending me to my death, I could never trust Lucy with anything. I just wanted to be an accepting mother, but look where it got me.

Tonight, I'm still reeling from seeing Lucy in that footage.

I plop down on the couch and find the TV remote to distract myself. As I cruise through the channels, a thought occurs to me. A sudden urge to contact Lucy washes over me, so I discard the remote and grab my phone instead. My phone is now over five years old (I should upgrade it), but it contains all my phone contacts, including Lucy's. I could reach her with my fingertips unless she's changed her phone number.

What are the odds she did that? Probably high, since she wanted to move on with her life and erase the part associated with her birth mother—me.

I open my phone. There she is: Lucy Davis. Of course, she doesn't have my or Jimmy's last name, since she got adopted as a baby.

I click on "send a text message," staring at the empty screen for God knows how long. My hands tremble, because I've forgotten what's appropriate to say in a text message.

The more I think about whether I should proceed, the more I'm convinced I should. Lucy owes me answers. Not just for witnessing Jimmy tampering with my car brakes, but she also needs to explain what on earth gave her the right to give up my home to another family, if that's what she's done.

She's going to get a big surprise when she meets me. The new Lynn. Everyone is.

I don't know if time alone gave me another perspective in life, but I've come out more confident and stronger. Better resolved. No one can mess with the new Lynn. I now consider myself a warrior. A survivor, against all odds.

Besides reading books, my other constant pastime was the gym, lifting and getting myself in shape. I'm approaching sixty, but look more like I'm in my forties. If Lucy saw me again, she'd be shocked.

I type a message:

> It's Lynn. I am out of jail. We need to talk.

I read it repeatedly for the content and the tone. The simpler the better. No feelings added. No emojis. I'm wondering if I should put down 'your mom' next to my name, but I change my mind. I've gotta be the only jailed Lynn she knows.

My nerves start to get the better of me, and I hesitate. I'm a changed woman, but I still fear that Lucy will retaliate in the worst possible ways. What if she curses me out?

That very last conversation with my old dealer friend, Skull, pushes its way into my mind. I'd paid him a visit before he called the cops on me. When I told him I didn't trust Lucy, I suggested I make her disappear, push her off the cliff into the ocean, make it look like an accident. What if he'd told her about that conversation? Surely, it would make anyone go insane.

Despite the flicker of doubt igniting inside me, I gather all my wits and finally push 'send'.

My eyes widen in anticipation, but the chime sound comes in faster than I expected.

It's an undeliverable message notification. My text cannot be delivered. This phone number no longer belongs to her, and I cannot reach her.

Part of me is relieved, because I'm still not ready to face Lucy. But the less accessible she seems, the more my desire to find her grows. The only person who can help is Andrew.

I open a new message and type:

> Andrew, I have another mission for you. Finding Lucy. Let's talk tomorrow.

The swooshing sound of sending the message is the only one in the room, sending a sliver of relief through me. I'm so grateful to have a private investigator as a friend.

Yes. Let's talk tomorrow, Lynn. Good
night and sweet dreams.

I turn on the TV and smile. I can't wait to find Lucy.

CHAPTER 4

FIRST THING IN THE MORNING, I make myself a strong coffee. The jail coffee had tasted like crap, and I could never get used to it, so I'd quit drinking it. Upon my return to the outside world, I relished the strong taste of the good stuff, enjoying the sudden rush to my head. All the small things I wasn't able to enjoy now feel glorious.

I go to the massive balcony, overlooking the ocean, and sit on a large chair that swings from the ceiling. The ocean sparkles with the rising sun, sending butterflies in my belly. This view is priceless. It's giving me serene vibes, and for the first time in a while, I feel there's a purpose in all this. I'm so lucky to be alive and breathing.

My plan is to kick the family out of my home as soon as possible. How do I do that? I take my phone out and google how to evict tenants. Reading the evictions laws in New Hampshire, I find it's not as complicated as I'd thought. All I need to do is give them a thirty-day notice in writing with a reason and deliver it in person.

Easy peasy.

I close the browser on my phone and go right to text messages.

Hey, do you have time for lunch today? Let's talk!

Andrew is on it already. Three dots are dancing on the text screen, and he responds with a resounding *yes*.

I open my browser again to see if Red Urchin is open today. Barbara rarely closed the restaurant when I worked there, but it's worth checking before showing up. It would be nice to visit my old stomping ground and see Barbara after so long. I've thought about her all these years and what she might be up to. Even though she was high strung, opinionated, and sometimes difficult, she had redeeming qualities. She gave me the waitressing job when I was at my lowest in life. It will be nice to see Barbara again.

But the message on the home page of their website, posted in April of this year, sends me into shock. My eyes dart across the words written in big bold letters:

As of July 1, Red Urchin will be permanently closed after 34 years of operations. We thank all our customers for being loyal all these years. We loved to cook for you and put smiles on all your faces. We believe we were an inte-

gral part of the Hampton community, and we thank you for your patronage.

However, our time at the restaurant has to come to an end. After long consideration, our family is moving to Florida, where we've always wanted to retire. We will miss the incredible community and interactions with many of you. Thank you again, and may God bless you.

I stare at the page for a long while, trying to process the information. Barbara has moved to Florida? I guess I won't be seeing her again. But it would have been nice to say goodbye.

Andrew will have to pick a meeting place for lunch. Hampton has changed little in five years, but I can't remember all the restaurants from the top of my head. I tell him I'd prefer a quiet place where we can talk.

That afternoon, we meet at a local coffee shop, Perfect Brews, near the beach. As I approach the place, a flood of memories flash over me from where I'd first met Andrew. I'd been so nervous and frightened, not knowing what to expect from our first meeting.

When I enter Perfect Brews, I see Andrew sitting in the far corner, looking down at his phone. Like the first time I ever saw him, I am taken away by his stance and demeanor. He looks authoritative and handsome, like he'd just walked out of an action movie.

I'm grateful he brings a smile to my face, especially during a time when I haven't many other reasons to smile. He lifts his head from his phone and stands up when he sees me approach. He's wearing a pair of shorts and a tank top, as if he's ready for a stroll on the beach.

"Hey," he says.

His eyes light up when he sees me. He gives me a big hug, and I welcome his embrace. His cologne smells spicy, with peppery notes that add a sense of heat or vibrancy. I inhale as I bury my face into his neck. His touch feels good.

I peel myself off him and we sit down across from each other.

"Hi." I give him a small smile. "Long time no see."

He laughs at my quip. We live close by and could see each other within minutes if needed. Andrew lives in North Hampton in a single-family house surrounded by golf courses. Golf is his passion, and he plans on spending a considerable amount of time playing the sport once he retires for good. He could retire today if he wanted to, but he isn't ready yet. He's made good money working as a private investigator, and his stock investment has been kind to his wallet. But his mind needs to keep churning. He loves solving cases and bringing them to a successful conclusion. Mine might be his last one before he retires.

"Did you sleep okay?" He looks at me with worry on his face.

"Yeah, not bad. All things considered."

He nods. "I get it. It can't be easy seeing that footage last night."

I shrug. "Nothing surprises me anymore."

We order food and drinks and chat about the weather until Andrew cocks his head to the side and says, "So, tell me. What can I do for you?"

I take a deep breath before I say anything and bite down on my lower lip. "Well, I tried to reach out to Lucy last night."

His eyes widen. "And?"

"Unsuccessful. My message was undeliverable, so I'm assuming she's changed her phone number."

"Yep. Been there, done that."

I smirk. He still feels guilty about disappearing on me five years ago, but I try to remind him it isn't the time to reflect on the past. What was done was done. Time to move on.

"Well, I need your help to find her. I tried to Google her last night, but I've come across a few Lucy Davises on the internet, and none of them are her."

Andrew leans forward and interlaces his fingers on the table. "I'll do my best, Lynn. But, as you know, it might take some time. She may have moved or gotten married, which means she probably doesn't go by Lucy Davis anymore."

"Yeah, I get it. I thought about it. Of course, I'll do some digging myself, since I really don't have much else to do during the day."

It's true—I don't need to work for the rest of my life, and unfortunately, I don't have any hobbies, never have, so I need to occupy my time somehow.

"Do your thing."

Our food and drinks arrive, and we dig in. After eating crappy food in the jail for years, I chew slowly and savor every bite. God knows how many times I went back to my jail cell hungry, because the kitchen didn't serve enough food on my plate, or it was so awful I could barely touch it. I comb through the lettuce on my plate and look up at Andrew. "I just feel that Lucy and I have unfinished business. She has some explaining to do."

"Agreed." Andrew nods.

"Not to mention that she gave up my home to some strangers without giving me any warning. It's infuriating."

"Well, if it's definitely her who's done that, she's certainly bold. But don't worry, I think I have some ideas on how to get started. Our first step is to reclaim your home and talk to people living there. If Lucy had anything to do with renting your home, then the owners should have her information. Or at least someone else who did it has her information."

"Good thinking." I like that Andrew is good-looking *and* smart.

"Let me dig more information about the family so we can get a better profile. Knowing who they are will tell us what kind of approach we should take with them when we visit."

"Sounds like a plan, Andrew. I'm so happy you can work on the case."

"Of course. I'll get to work right away."

CHAPTER 5

THE FOLLOWING MORNING, my phone chimes with a text. It's Andrew.

> I've got info on the family who lives in your house. Can you talk?

I dial Andrew right away. He picks up after two rings. His voice beams with energy and enthusiasm. Like me, he's a morning person.

"So, listen. I was able to find info about the family. You're gonna love this. The guy is a plastic surgeon, and his wife is a stay-at-home mom. Three kids. A five and a three-year-old, and a newborn."

My stomach tightens with nerves.

"Shit."

"What?"

"I can't kick out a family with a newborn. It's ... I want my home back, but I don't want to be a monster."

"You can discuss specifics with them when we go meet

them. I'm pretty sure they can afford a smooth transition into their new home. The guy is practically a millionaire. Born into money. I'll tell you more when I see you. So, don't overthink it. Okay?"

My shoulders sag with relief. "Sure. What else did you find out?"

"I'll tell you more when I see you. But off the cuff, nothing in their records suggests they are ... how should I say this? Difficult? When we go visit, I would expect a fairly cordial interaction."

"That all sounds good. I have an eviction notice typed up and printed. I'm ready to go." A surge of excitement flows through me at the though of seeing my home again.

"Excellent. How about we meet in front of the house at six this evening? Does that work?"

"Sure does. See you then."

I hang up, suddenly nervous and unsettled as my brief joy at the news begins to seep away. Even though Andrew has reassured me that everything should go splendidly with the family, something tells me it won't. Or maybe the anxiety is coming from the knowledge that I'm getting closer to knowing Lucy's whereabouts. These people will probably know where to find her.

While I wait for six to roll in, I stroll to the downtown area and visit a few stores. A boutique store with art supplies and a used bookstore. I've passed both a million times before but never entered, because I had no reason to.

All that will change soon. To continue the passion for reading I'd picked up in jail, I'm going to buy a pile of books I can bury my face in. I want to try painting, too. It's something I've always wanted to do, but never had a chance. It would have been impossible to attempt while living in that dingy place with Jimmy.

The ladies at the stores seem pleasant and chatty. Now I've established myself in their circle, I will visit the stores more frequently and seek distraction from boredom.

The sky's the limit.

I arrive at the house before six and find Andrew's car parked out front. The house—my home—the little mansion by the ocean is looking grand, and for a second, I can't believe it's mine. I didn't get to live there for long, but while I did, it was the most wonderful experience. One I hope to live again.

I slide into Andrew's car and sit in the passenger seat.

Andrew is sitting at the steering wheel and talking on the phone. He hangs up and looks at me. "Hey there."

"You're early," I say, my forehead creased.

"So are you."

We stare at each other and burst out laughing. Andrew says, "I guess that's cool, because I can tell you more about the family before we knock on their door."

"Do tell." I lean closer, eager to hear.

"Like I said, Gabriel, the plastic surgeon, is filthy rich and seems to have a clean background. Both he and his wife grew up in Montana. They met in high school and have been together since. Three small children."

"And you said she was a stay-at-home mom?"

"Yes. But she has an interesting background. Her

father is a big shot in Montana. A military general. Rumors have it he has threatened Gabriel to cut his balls off if anything happened to his daughter. Apparently, she's an only child."

"Wow. Has he ever done anything to warrant the threat?" It sounds like the family has some interesting characters. Can't wait to meet these two!

"I don't know. I couldn't find any info. Apparently, he's been a surgeon for less than a decade now. His residence was a lot longer than the norm, as he wasn't ready to transition to a full-time physician." He pauses as if for dramatic effect. "And the most shocking part? Two of his patients had succumbed to the procedure and died, somewhat skewing his reputation among his colleagues and patients alike."

A long breath whistles out of me.

"And here's the best part," he continues. "Gabriel and his little crew move so frequently that kicking them out probably won't be an issue. But that's all I could find. There's no clear connection between him and Lucy. No past real estate transactions. No signed lease. Absolutely nothing. This is why our visit is crucial. We need Gabriel to speak."

I nod slowly, taking it all in. "Anything more about his wife?"

"She's some kinda wanna-be influencer on Instagram, but her posts don't have anything personal."

I don't know much about Instagram, but I'm curious. "What does she post about?"

"Mostly about make-up. And bras." Andrew nods and turns his head in embarrassment.

I laugh at him and grab his hand. "Are we ready?"

"Sure." He nods.

As we exit the car, I take a better peek at the house. The front lawn is adorned with a jungle gym, a slide, and a trampoline with some other toys scattered around. In the farther distance, just beyond the house, I hear voices of young children coming from the poolside. They're clearly home.

I stop by the gate, Andrew by my side. "Ready?" he asks.

"As ready as can be."

I appreciate Andrew's confidence. For the time I've known him, I don't think I've seen him looking nervous once.

We ring the bell on the gate and wait. I fidget, craning my neck toward the house, wondering what's taking so long. Andrew smiles at me, probably noticing how nervous I look. I lift my arm to check the time on my watch, and the seconds' hand seems to drag around.

I'm about to reach for the bell again when Andrew meets my hand mid-air and takes it gently in his. "Hey, hey, hey. Relax. Don't be nervous."

I shake my head. "I'm not. I just don't understand why they're so slow." I roll my eyes for good measure.

Seconds later, a woman holding a baby walks across the yard in our direction. She looks young and vibrant. Her long blonde hair is tied in a high ponytail. She's wearing a sleeveless dress and flip-flops, and she's all muscles. As she gets closer, I notice her fingernails are sporting a French manicure and a diamond ring the size of my kidney. It sparkles against the sun.

The baby in her hands looks content. I can tell that she's taking good care of the baby. The woman's forehead creases as she gets closer, and she says, "Can I help you, folks?"

Andrew and I exchange looks, and I nod at him, giving him permission to speak. Better him than me. I'm a little rusty on all the social protocols, plus, I imagine receiving an eviction notice from a handsome, confident man would be a lot easier to handle than it would be from a short, older woman.

"Hi, my name is Andrew. This is Lynn."

"Hi."

She looks confused, but she stays put and appears to entertain the possibility of learning more about why we're here.

"So, Lynn Miller here is my client and has just returned to society after years of being away." Andrew clears his throat. "Well, when she returned, she discovered that a family—well, you—occupied her home, and now she would like to reclaim it."

The woman stares at both of us with wide eyes before granting us a skeptical frown. I'd brought the deed of the house with my name on it and my ID in case I need to prove the ownership. Her look of distrust suggests I might need to, but I hope I won't have to.

"Really? Where have you been all these years?"

She still looks shocked, but her voice remains calm.

There's no reason to beat around the bush. I tell her like it is. "I was in jail."

"Jail?"

"Yeah, jail. I got out, like, a week ago."

She chews her lip and looks from Andrew to me. "What were you in the jail for?"

"I killed my husband."

My voice is steady as I stare deep into the woman's eyes.

"Oh, wow." She gazes down at the ground as if she's thinking. Andrew and I exchange looks, and I wonder how she's about to react. She looks up again and gives me another wide-eyed stare. "Oh my God, you're that woman who won the lottery, right?"

I nod and smile. I think I like this woman. She's unfazed by the fact I'm a murderer.

"That's right," I tell her. "That was five years ago."

She approaches the gate, unlocks it, opening it wide. "Come in. I'd always wanted to meet you."

I suppress a chuckle, surprised at her reaction.

She stands by the gate, watching the baby flap his hands around, then she turns around and walks toward the house. Andrew and I trail behind her in eerie silence. As we cross the yard, memories flood through me. The very last minutes I spent here were in a gruesome attempt to get away from the cops. Skull had just ratted me out, and I'd plunged into the ocean, hoping they wouldn't catch me. I was so naïve. And afraid. Very much so.

I shake my head to dislodge the unease and concentrate on our hostess's hospitality. So far, so good. If she's as welcoming as she seems, it shouldn't be a problem kicking them out of the house.

Just as I think that, our hostess extends her arm toward the house and says, "Welcome! Make yourselves at home."

CHAPTER 6

EVERYTHING LOOKS the same as before, except the hedges leading up to the cliff are much taller and bushier.

I look around and notice the house is in good shape. No need for major repairs or painting.

The pool on the side is sparkling in the sun. Two little kids are splashing inside, having fun, and a sliver of guilt washes over me when I realize I would soon evict them. Do they call this their true home? Or is it just temporary?

"Why don't we sit over there?" She points at the round table with shade by the pool. Yes, that's the table Lucy and I used to sit at and simmer in silence. "You got here right on time. He's just about to fall asleep."

She points at the baby, whose little teeth show when he yawns widely. The other two kids pay us no attention at all.

"My husband should be home soon. I'm sure he'll be more than happy to meet you." She offers a small smile.

We all sit around the table, and Andrew gazes at me as

if making sure I'm okay. I'm fine, even though it's still strange that someone else has claimed my home as theirs.

It just doesn't feel right.

"Oh, I almost forgot." She laughs, revealing her perfectly white, straight teeth. She points at herself first, then at each of the kids. "I'm sorry. I'm Charlotte, that's Sebastian, that one is Alexander, and this is Oliver." She kisses baby Oliver on the cheek.

I appreciate the introduction and her friendly nature. But how did she know about me?

She looks at me. "You're Lynn Miller, right? I've seen the news reports about you, and I've always wondered what you're like—and I finally get to meet you." She looks at me like I am a celebrity.

Both winning the lottery and killing my husband have made me infamous in town. So many stories have circulated about my life and past, but the buzz has surely died down by now. Most people don't seem to recognize me. My photos in the media all looked terrible. I looked unkempt. My eyes were drooping. My skin, rough. If there's one mugshot of a murderer you want to show to new cops-in-training, it would be mine. A perfect picture of a lowlife.

It's amazing what a little more confidence and self-belief do to your appearance. I look a lot better since I've taken care of myself mentally and physically in jail. It's ironic, because some people rot in there, their soul and mind eaten alive. But not me. As for me, I had already hit rock bottom—there was no deeper place to sink.

So, it's no surprise people don't recognize me anymore. I'm a new Lynn, and I love the new me.

And it makes me wonder again: how did Charlotte recognize me immediately? It's a scary thought.

I nod. "Yep. You got it. I'm Lynn Miller."

A pinch of uneasiness washes over me, but I put my thoughts to the side. I don't have time to dwell on it. I'm here to investigate Lucy's whereabouts and, well, eventually kick the family out.

The baby falls asleep in Charlotte's arms, and she stands up to put him in his crib. I wonder what room she has chosen for him.

Before she leaves the patio, she says, "My husband should be home soon. He's on his way, but he's hitting some traffic."

With that, Andrew and I stay behind on the patio, darting our eyes between the kids and the far distance into the ocean. We're silent, but my mind is churning, contemplating things. Why are they renting a house as opposed to buying one? Sure, they seem fine people on the outside, but I bet if you dig deeper, there could be some sinister secrets beneath them.

Charlotte disrupts my thoughts by stomping down the stairs.

"The boy is already asleep." She lets out a hearty laugh. "My husband should be here any time. Would you like something to drink?"

Andrew and I shake our heads in unison. We're not here to socialize.

"No," I confirm. "We're here because we need to get more information about the person who rented my house to you."

Charlotte scratches her cheek and gazes down before looking up again. "Okay."

I look at Andrew and see that his squinty eyes are boring into hers. It gives me more confidence to know that Andrew is here. Without a doubt, he will intervene if I make a mistake or say something foolish.

"We need to know the name of the person who rented the house to you. And bonus points if you have their contact information or know where they are."

"Oh." Charlotte's eyes widen. "Well, I'd be happy to help, but I wasn't much involved with a house search. We'll just have to wait for my husband. He should be home—"

A man in his mid-forties walks from around the corner of the house. The kids glance at him as he arrives, but stay in the pool and keep splashing around. Charlotte's face lights up and she jumps on her feet to greet him. "Hi, babe."

They hug, and the man stares at us over her shoulders. His eyebrows stitch together as if wondering who we are and what we're doing on his patio. Little does he know the patio is not really his. But he will find out soon.

He releases himself from her hug and looks at her. "Who do we have here, darling?"

Charlotte suddenly looks a little flustered. "Oh, let me

introduce you. This is Lynn, and that's Andrew. Lynn owns this house."

She turns to us and points at her husband. "This is Gabriel."

While Charlotte smiles, Gabriel's face hardens, and the spark of curiosity in his eyes dims to a cold glare. "What can we help you with, folks?" His voice is raspy and stiff, as if he hasn't spoken all day.

I look at Andrew, and Andrew gives me a small nod.

I swallow and force myself to look them in the eyes. "We're here to give you an evection notice. And ask you a few questions about the person who rented this house."

CHAPTER 7

GABRIEL'S FACE PALES, and his glare deepens. I'm sure he wants to kick back and relax at "home" after a long day at work. He says nothing and sits at the table, staring at Andrew and me. Before my jail time, I'd have found his behavior intimidating, but now, I just find it plain annoying. Who does he think he is?

"Where's the proof you own this house?" His gaze remains trained on us, as if calculating every move we make, every word we utter.

I put a copy of the deed on the table. "Here."

He first looks at me, then the piece of paper, and grabs it. His eyes dart all over the page, and then widen as he slowly shakes his head.

"Got it," Gabriel says. "Well, it's your lucky day, because we're moving to Texas in a month."

Charlotte snaps her head and looks at him. Moving to Texas seems like a surprise to her. And, if her expression is anything to go by, not a good one. Her eyes glisten with sudden tears, and she places her head down as if to avoid the stares. It's obvious this relationship doesn't have a healthy balance, but I shouldn't be one to judge. Been there, done that. A pang of sadness washes over me for Charlotte. She seems a little clueless about life.

"Oh, you are?" I have to say something. A shot of relief surges through me. At least I'll get my home back without too much drama.

"Yes. My profession is such that I move a lot. At least in the first decade of my career. Our lease expires in a month, but we will move a week earlier. You can have the place all for yourself."

He looks at the house and scans it, as if he's scrutinizing it for the first time.

"Well, great! That makes things easy."

I look at Andrew, and he smiles. It's almost as if he's checking off an item from his impossible-to-do list in his head.

But now, I must get to the tough part of questioning. My heart picks up a beat, and my palms sweat. Any thought or mention of Lucy brings out a cocktail of emotions. Memories, good and bad, flash through my eyes. Her betrayal stings, but I'm here to get to the task at hand and try to find her.

"Can you tell me who rented the house?"

My voice comes out a little shaky, and I cross my leg over the other, clearing my throat. I want to appear in control, but those pesky memories keep stabbing my heart.

"Why is that important?" Gabriel asks with narrowed eyes.

"Why?" I repeat. "Well, whoever rented the house did not have my permission to do so. I think, at the least, I need to have a talk with the person."

"Hah," he says. "Where were you when we rented the house?"

Here we go again. I hate repeating myself, but I dive in. "I was in jail for murder. I killed my husband five years ago, then was let go after fresh evidence surfaced."

We now have a staring contest, and I notice him swallow hard.

"So, unfortunately, I wasn't here to stop the renting from happening. Do you mind sharing who rented the house to you?"

"Oh, sure." He runs his hand over his luscious hair.

Charlotte peers eagerly at him as if waiting for a response. Andrew's antennas are up, too, clearly hoping for a big breakthrough.

"It was a few years ago. I'm not sure I can remember her full name." He stares in the ocean's direction and squints as if he's thinking hard.

"Her name?" A good sign. It's a she. But surely, he'd know who they were making regular payments to? Something feels off.

Charlotte looks like she wants to chime in, but Gabriel gives her a stern look she seems to be familiar with. She stays quiet and fixes her gaze on the table in front of her.

Gabriel seems to be unearthing his memories. He

closes his eyes and shakes his head. Then he looks out in a distance, "It was a younger woman, if I remember correctly, and she was a real estate agent at the Hampton Realty."

Hope sparks inside me. *This is it.* We've found Lucy. All we need is her new phone number and we're on the way.

"So, her name is Lucy?" I offer.

"No, no. I don't think it's Lucy." Gabriel frowns. "It was Suzanne something. But I can't remember her last name." He scoffs. "I can't remember what I had for lunch yesterday."

He's the only one laughing at his quip. Charlotte keeps her gaze aimed downward and says nothing.

"Suzanne?" Andrew says. "Could it be Lucy instead, by any chance?"

Gabriel looks at Andrew and slowly shakes his head while appearing to be thinking. "Lucy? Doesn't ring the bell. And she is definitely down as a Suzanne in my phone contacts."

"Here's the thing," Andrew chimes in. "It's very important that we speak to Suzanne. Do you think you can give us her phone number?"

Without hesitation, Gabriel pulls his phone out of his shirt pocket. "Yeah, no problem. Anything to help."

He dictates Suzanne's phone number, and we both take note. Andrew and I exchange looks and smile, happy that we're getting somewhere. Hopefully, when we call Suzanne, she'll know who Lucy is.

This is easier than I thought. I sigh, and as I get up to leave, Andrew follows me.

"Well, thank you for everything. I will see you in less than a month to take the keys and see you out."

"Sure." Gabriel nods.

"Until then, enjoy your stay." I turn to Charlotte and cock my head in sympathy. "It was really nice to meet you, dear."

With that, Andrew and I storm across the front yard, filled with excitement about our next steps. As we trudge through my lawn, I feel Gabriel's mean eyes boring into my back.

But I don't really care. We just got a big break. We've finally found Lucy.

CHAPTER 8

ANDREW IS DRIVING ME HOME, all smiles. "Well, that was easy."

The weather is gorgeous, and butterflies flutter in my belly. It's a delightful feeling to embrace freedom again, though part of me still feels like I'm being held back by something or someone. Those hollowing sounds between the jail walls still course through my veins. But I try to dismiss the feeling. I am here. Now.

My elbow hangs out of the window while my hair flaps around. Despite the calm and the hope from moments ago, a flicker of unease stirs something inside me, and I fidget in my seat.

"Hey, Andrew, did you notice something weird about the couple?"

He turns to me for a second. "What? That he's a complete control freak?"

"I mean, yes, that, too. But that's not what I mean." I

play with my fingers as I think about our interactions with them. "Neither one was surprised to see me. Plus, they looked like they knew about me all along. Not to mention that they're moving in less than a month. Isn't that a strange coincidence?"

Andrew shrugs his shoulders while looking straight behind the wheel. "I don't know. Maybe they're curious about you. You were on the news."

"Yeah, I guess." I pause as I stare out the window, thinking. "I don't know. That whole interchange was kind of weird. But I'm glad I'll get my house back soon."

"Yeah, that's a good thing."

"So ... will you be calling Suzanne?"

He nods. "Yes. As soon as I get home, I'll be doing some investigation. Gabriel didn't give us her last name, but it can't be hard to locate a Suzanne at the Hampton Realty."

I smile. Any step closer to Lucy means getting closure sooner. I can't wait to hear what Andrew has come up with. He drops me off at my apartment and tells me he'll call me as soon as he finds out something—anything—about Suzanne and Lucy.

When I arrive home, I'm feeling antsy. I could just as easily do my own searching, but I decide against it. Andrew will do it all, and he knows what he's doing.

I sit on the balcony and watch the ocean sparkle from a distance. Maybe I should read the book I'd bought at the bookstore today. I've never read Stephen King (yes, I'm ashamed to say this), but I'd love to give him a whirl. I'm about to stand up, but a force glues me to the couch. I realize I'm tired, so I close my eyes, and the fresh air lulls me to sleep.

Half an hour must have gone by when my phone wakes me up. It's Andrew.

"Hi," I say, sleepy.

"Did I wake you up?"

"You did, but no worries."

Ever since I got out of jail, I'm a lot more relaxed: no noise coming from neighboring cells, no guards angrily slamming the doors, no howling sounds waking me at night ... my body must be catching up to normalcy.

"Can you meet me somewhere? I want to tell you what I discovered."

"Oh. You can't tell me over the phone?"

That's either a good or a really bad sign.

Andrew is silent until he lets out a little laugh. "I could, but I'd rather see you."

Andrew knows what to say and when. I don't mind seeing him, either. As I find my bearings and establish myself all over again, I realize that being alone isn't my favorite.

Half an hour later, we find ourselves having dinner at a new restaurant along the main road, right across from the beach. The dim lighting inside sets a warm, intimate atmosphere, and I notice several couples dining. It's the kind of place where romance might blossom into lifelong adventures.

Andrew has a poker face, and I can't tell if he's about to tell me good or bad news.

He leans forward at the table and looks at me, his eyes darting all over.

I let out a nervous chuckle. "Okay, I'm dying to find out what you've got."

He gazes down at the table, then looks up. "Well, it's not looking good."

I lean against the chair, feeling as if someone stabbed me in the heart. Just hearing the words "not looking good," dissipates my hope, and I feel deflated. But maybe it's not as bad as it sounds? I await Andrew's next words.

"I called Suzanne, and her phone didn't seem to work. It got disconnected or something. Not sure. Then I searched for a Suzanne associated with the Hampton Realty, but nothing came up. Absolutely nothing."

That feels like a punch in the gut.

"Could Gabriel have been wrong? Did he give us a wrong name or phone number?"

"Well, that's the thing," Andrew says. "I called Hampton Realty, and they told me that, yes, there was a Suzanne working there about a year ago, but she's no longer there. When I pressed for more information, I didn't get far. The person told me they don't know where she is or how to get in touch with her."

I gasp. This is terrible news.

"I did get her last name, but upon further search, I didn't get far at all."

"What is her last name?"

"It's Kaminsky. Sounds like Polish origin."

I roll my eyes involuntarily, feeling dizzy from all of this. Feeling ill, I press further. "So, when you searched under Suzanne Kaminsky, nothing came up?"

Andrew nods. "Absolutely nothing. And it's quite strange. I really don't understand at all."

CHAPTER 9

WHEN I COME HOME, I decide to see it for myself that Suzanne Kaminsky is nowhere to be found.

All my stuff is hopefully still in the mansion, but I don't have access to it. Andrew has loaned me his old laptop until I can reclaim my home. I place the computer on my lap and open the search browser. I type in two words that are now haunting me:

Suzanne Kaminsky

Not much comes up.

There's an obituary for Suzanne Kaminsky from a decade ago, so that couldn't be it. I scroll down and locate another Suzanne Kaminsky; this one is a history professor somewhere in California. That can't be it, either.

There is definitely no real estate agent called Suzanne Kaminsky. And I'm puzzled by this. Did Gabriel intentionally give us a wrong name or phone number?

I put the computer down in defeat. Obviously, neither Suzanne nor Lucy can be located. Which means Andrew and I need to rethink our strategy. I wonder if Lucy still lives in New Hampshire. If she does, does she ever come around? Perhaps to check on the house or visit her old neighbors?

An idea comes to mind, and I go to bed, hopeful yet again. When I wake up tomorrow morning, my plan is to have breakfast, caffeinate myself enough to function throughout the day, and head over to my old stomping ground. Maybe Rose, my old neighbor, knows something.

Rose usually knows everything.

———

At six in the morning, I'm already up.

I hum through my nose as I buzz around in the kitchen, preparing breakfast. I love those early mornings where everything is so calm, and half the town is still asleep. The ocean in the distance is a beautiful backdrop to my mood. I feel alive and invigorated.

We may not be even close to finding Lucy, but I feel everything will play out well.

By seven, I'm already out the door. The beach is empty, but several people are jogging and getting their exercise in. I park on the main street and decide to walk a couple of blocks. It will get the jitters out of me as I breathe in the fresh ocean breeze. Besides, it's nice to see the place again, through a fresh set of eyes.

Everything looks the same, yet it feels different. It's like old memories are being suppressed and replaced by my new feelings. It's been over five years since I set foot in this part of my old town. The casino, my favorite place once upon a time, looks the same from the outside. I don't dare check what it looks like inside. Gambling is now in my distant past, and I don't want to revisit it.

New establishments have replaced some of the older restaurants. In the summer, these spots are packed with tourists from all over the world.

I turn around the corner and find myself on that familiar street.

The street where I lived with my husband for decades.

I stop in my tracks to compose myself. Upon seeing my old home, memories flood my mind. All the fights Jimmy and I had. All the beatings he unleashed on me. The constant fear and paranoia.

I'm having a hard time breathing, but I close my eyes and take slow, deep breaths. When I open them again, I scrutinize the place more closely and notice that it differs vastly from how I remember it. For one, it doesn't look like a trashy place with broken roof tiles and a pile of garbage in the back. Lilac and Azalea bushes and Shasta Daisies decorate the front.

Whoever lives there takes care of the property. The grass is finely curated, and the house looks decent. Nothing like the way it looked back in the day.

On the other hand, Rose's house is starkly different from before. It's almost as if our houses got swapped.

I remember Rose spending a crazy amount of time in her yard, taking care of her flowers, watering them religiously, cutting the grass twice a week. Everything looked so perfect that it almost seemed intimidating. That was her way of spending time in the yard and conspicuously spying on her neighbors, learning what everyone was up to.

Now, some flowers looked dry, the grass overgrown, the metal on the front metal door corroded. I wonder if the condition of her garden resembled her state of mind. That's how it usually goes. Is Rose even still alive?

The only way to find out is to knock on her door.

As I walk through the metal door, my heart pumps. Facing Rose is like seeing an old family member you had a falling out with but loved very much. With family, forgiveness is key. I just hope, when she sees me, she will be receptive to me.

I knock on the door and wait. When we lived next door, we often didn't knock; we'd let ourselves in. I would do the same now, but I don't even know if Rose still lives here. She could be living in senior housing or staying with a family member who would take care of her, because she has to be in her eighties now.

I stand for a minute before I knock on the door again. On the other side of the door, a raspy voice travels out. "Just a second."

The voice sounds tired and strained. But that's Rose. That voice is undeniable. I could only imagine what she looks like in old age, but I smile, because suddenly I'm looking forward to seeing her bright face again.

The door opens, and Rose peeks through a small opening.

What used to be a bundle of energy is now a diminished figurine standing in front of me. She appears a lot shorter and a hump on her back has grown twice in size. Her hair is completely gray, and her face is full of wrinkles.

She sees me, but I can tell by the look on her face that she doesn't recognize me. If she hears my voice, maybe she will.

"Hi, Rose."

Judging from her deep stare, I gather she still doesn't recognize me.

"Can I help you?"

"It's me. Lynn. Your old neighbor." I chuckle nervously.

Her brows stitch together, as if contemplating my answer.

This is going terribly.

"Who?"

"Lynn Miller." I point my hand at my old house. "Remember? I used to live in that house, right next door?"

Her eyes dart all over me, and I think the message is catching up. Her mouth falls open.

"Lynn?" she whispers. "Lynn. Is that really you?"

I nod and reassure her it's really me.

"Come on in." She extends her arm. "I've been waiting for you for years."

CHAPTER 10

I WALK through the door and find myself in Rose's messy abode. Unopened mail is scattered all over the floor, food leftovers sit on the table, and her sweaters and shirts hang over the TV. The air smells heavy and musty. I hold my breath and scrunch my nose. All the windows are shut, and the curtains are drawn, making the house feel like a coffin. It looks like death in the making.

It strikes me as strange, since Rose used to be a neat freak. When Jimmy and I first moved in as a young couple, she came over to help me organize my tiny closet.

What has happened to Rose?

"Sit down, dear."

She points at the couch in the corner, adorned with a bunch of pillows. I push all the stuff away and make myself at home. When I sit down and take a breath, I notice only then how Rose inches along at a painful pace. Her feet shuffle while she holds onto pieces of furniture for balance on her way to the chair. I want to get up and help her, but it looks like this is a new way of living for Rose, and she might be embarrassed. I don't say anything.

She finally makes it to the chair and sits down, sighing loudly, as if tired from making several steps back from the door. Something about her demeanor has changed. Her face looks sullen and sad. She sits in a chair across from me, with her movements slow and difficult, and looks at me with wide eyes. Her body shrinks into the seat, and the hump on her back looks bigger as she leans forward.

"I'm sorry about this mess. I haven't been feeling so good lately." Her speech has slowed. It's amazing what five years can do to a person. Rose definitely needs care.

"No worries. It's good to see you, Rose."

"Good to see you, too." She folds her arm on the armrest and buries her cheek in her hand, as if she's about to fall asleep. "Where have you been, Lynn?"

"I was ... away," I say, as I avert my eyes from her. "I've had rough few years, but I am back."

I choose not to say anything about my jail time. It doesn't seem like it would make much difference to Rose.

"That's good. Well, you've missed a lot of fun stuff around here." Rose perks up a little and sits straighter in the chair.

"Oh. Like what?"

"Well, the couple next door just had a baby. A tiny, tiny baby. A beautiful baby boy. They came to visit me the other day. He's so ..." Rose makes a space between her hands and continues. "...tiny."

That doesn't sound like something I'd miss out on, but

I don't say anything.

"That's pretty exciting."

"Oh! Do you want something to drink? How rude I haven't offered anything." Her mouth opens in an 'O'.

"I'm good. I just came by to say hello and see how you've been."

She looks at me and nods continuously in silence. Things are turning awkward, as if she can sense my agenda for the visit isn't as straightforward as I'm making out. I'm here primarily to find out if Lucy might have made an appearance recently, or if Rose might have stumbled on her somehow. It's a long shot, but I've got nothing to lose. Our options are drying up.

I interlace my fingers and crack my knuckles.

"Did anyone else come visit you recently, Rose?"

She stitches her eyebrows and purses her lips. "Like who?"

I swallow. "Has Lucy come to see you at all?"

She frowns. "Lucy?"

"Yeah, Lucy. Remember my daughter?" I chuckle.

Her eyes light up. "Of course! Lucy."

My shoulders relax.

"Has she come to see you at all?"

"Yes, of course. She's come a few times in the past few months."

My heart wants to jump out of my chest. So, Lucy is around, after all! She has come by to see Rose, and I hope she's left some evidence behind her about how she might be contacted. Maybe a phone number? Because who wouldn't offer their phone number to an old lady in case she needed help or urgent care, right?

"What a wonderful child you have." Rose smiles as if she's reminiscing about her interactions with Lucy.

"When was the last time she came by?" I keep my voice as casual as I can manage.

"Oh. Let's see." She squints and scratches her temple. "A couple of weeks ago? She came by and sat there ... yeah, exactly where you're sitting. She was telling me she just got a job at the ice cream shop around the corner. She ... she looks happy."

I devour every word she says as adrenaline flies through my veins. I almost want to jump out of my seat and run to the shop, but I stifle the urge.

"The ice cream shop, eh?" I sound nonchalant, but a storm is brewing inside me. I'm as close to finding Lucy as I could be. I know exactly what ice cream shop Rose is referring to.

"Yes. She told me to stop by, and she'd treat me to a cone. Wonderful, wonderful child."

While Rose talks, despite her smile, her voice remains monotonous. Not an ounce of excitement injected. And that makes me wary. Something seems to be amiss.

"When did she say she'd stop by again?"

"She didn't say."

I nod, not sure what else to ask.

"Now I remember," Rose says, looking into a distance, her eyes glazing over. "Jimmy came by yesterday to say hi."

My blood freezes. "Jimmy?"

"Yes. He came by and gave me a big hug. You know, he always was like my son." Rose shakes her head as she stares into a distance.

Doesn't she know Jimmy is dead?

"You don't mean my husband, Jimmy? Do you, Rose?"

She stiffens. "What do you mean?"

"Are you saying my husband, Jimmy, came to visit?" My voice has crept up an octave.

"Yes, yes. I don't know any other Jimmy!" She raises her voice in defense.

Rose has completely lost her mind. If she believes dead Jimmy came to visit her, could all this stuff about Lucy coming to visit be true? I have my doubts.

Feeling defeated, I decide it's time for me to leave. I stand up, and Rose frowns. "Where are you going, dear?"

I look at my watch as if to state the urgency. "I'm meeting someone in fifteen minutes. But I'll be back soon."

I wouldn't mind stopping by occasionally to check up on Rose.

"That sounds good. You should come with Jimmy next time. You're my favorite couple."

I cringe and say nothing.

On my way to the car, I shake my head, upset about how steeply Rose has declined and nearly lost her marbles.

For good measure, I stop by the ice cream shop, just in case. It doesn't hurt to try.

When I enter the shop, it's nearly empty. A teenage girl greets me from behind the counter.

"Hi. How can I help?"

"Hi," I whisper, afraid someone may eavesdrop. "I'm not here for ice cream."

The girl's smile disappears, and confusion arrives on her face. "So, how can I help?"

"Do you happen to know a ... Lucy?" I keep my voice low.

Her face brightens. "Like, Lucy Score, the romance author?"

I shake my head and smile. "No, no. Not that Lucy. I'm talking about a woman in her late twenties who I think might have worked here."

The girl's face is a roller-coaster of emotions. Now she looks perplexed and sad all at once. "No, I don't know any other Lucy. Sorry." She shrugs her shoulders.

I suppress a frown. What has her looking so upset? "Do you know if any Lucy has worked here at all?"

"No." She shakes her head. "I've worked here every summer for the past few years, and I never met a Lucy."

Before I leave the shop, I get myself a cup of chocolate ice cream with hot fudge and sprinkles on top. It's been a while since I had a good dessert. I head to the beach to take a walk and clear my thoughts. The beach is lovely. I park myself close to the ocean and sit on the warm sand, thinking of what my next steps should be. I really don't know. Lucy seems to have fallen through the earth and can't be found.

A chilling thought creeps through me. Could she be dead? Andrew would find out, no doubt.

CHAPTER 11

I PULL my phone out of my pocket and text Andrew:

> I am at the beach if you want to join me.

Andrew either golfs with his buddies in the afternoon, immerses himself in his private investigation business, or nothing. I get a text back a minute later, so I must have caught him while doing nothing.

> I will be there in thirty minutes. Save me a spot.

I'm desperate for Andrew's help. And his company.

To still my racing thoughts about Lucy, I get up to take a short walk down the sidewalk by the beach. It's beautiful at this time of week and day—fewer people around to pollute the view. I remember my younger days when I'd get up at a wee hour and go to the beach for a swim. There's nothing like being young, when nothing seems like too much trouble to do or accomplish. Lucky for me, Andrew likes to surf and spend time on his boat, so I foresee many days ahead of me in the ocean, enjoying the scenery.

As I set foot on the curb, someone calls me.

"Lynn?"

The voice sounds awfully familiar, and my brain scans for answers, but I just can't figure out who it belongs to.

Then again. "Lynn!"

I turn in the voice's direction and face a young man who's looking up at me from a wheelchair. His hair is unkempt, and his eyes are droopy.

When he calls my name again and tells me his, I freeze. Now I remember him (how could I forget?)

Danny. The cop.

"Lynn, remember me?"

I gasp, "Danny. I could hardly recognize you. But yes, I remember you." Of his young stature, only his eyes have remained the same. He looks beat.

He casts a wide smile. "Glad to see you."

I say nothing, because I'm not sure I feel the same.

"I heard you got out of jail recently."

I wonder where he'd heard that, but Hampton is small, and people talk. No doubt, word has spread around.

I nod. "That's right. My PI found some surveillance tapes to prove that Jimmy had messed with my brakes. I guess it's not the rats who chewed on the brakes after all." I say in a bitter tone. "And my attorney is a miracle worker who got me out."

"Yeah, I heard." He gazes down, then looks up again, guilt etched in his expression. "Listen, Lynn, I need to tell you something, but it's quite upsetting."

I raise my brow in anticipation. "Yeah? Nothing really surprises me anymore, Danny. I've lived through it all. But sure, tell me. What is it?"

He looks around and watches a few people standing by. He wheels himself toward me and stops at my feet.

Danny whispers, "The prosecutors knew about the tape before your sentence. But they chose not to present it."

My fists clench and unclench instantly, and my jaw tightens. Besides Lucy, a slew of other people wanted me in jail, I guess. It makes me crazy to know this. And I don't even want to know how they got a hold of the tape. It's strange that someone would dig it up only to hide it and strengthen their case against me.

"Remember James, the cop?" Danny continues.

Oh, yes. *James.*

James used to patrol around my home all the time, snooping on me, stalking my every step. I never figured out why or what he wanted from me, but I think I'm about to hear it all.

"James was the mastermind behind all this. He and Jimmy exchanged favors in the past, and when Jimmy died, he swore by his life he'd send you to jail. He blamed you for everything, even though he knew what Jimmy did. But the rest of us couldn't do shit, because James was a powerful figure in the police department. He was a bit of a bully, you know."

My vision blurs, and my stomach lurches. "Where is he now?"

"I've heard he moved down to South Carolina to retire. Someone said he couldn't take the harsh winters here anymore." He shrugs. "Anyway, story over."

I gaze at Danny, noticing one of his legs is missing. "So, what happened to you?"

He looks down at his legs. "Oh, this?"

He's so young, and it must be a huge adjustment for him to be using a wheelchair.

"It was a cross-fire accident. I thought it could only happen in movies. But here I am!"

"I'm so sorry, Danny."

"Thanks, Lynn. Hey, listen, I wish you all the best. And I'm sorry for everything you've gone through."

"It's okay, Danny. And take care." I really am okay. I can say that now, because I'm happy about where I am in my life. And that's the worst punishment for my past foes.

CHAPTER 12

I SIT on the beach for a long while, contemplating the chance encounter I'd just had with Danny. Poor fellow. I feel bad for him, but I find it ironic how things have played out in my life.

For the majority of the time, I was making mistake after mistake, surrounded by bad people, leading to the ultimate fate of ending up in jail. I was like a magnet to bad things. I've heard once some people are born like that. They attract bad luck and shitty people. And it becomes a vicious cycle you can't jump out of.

Between drug use, a mediocre life, giving up my daughter at birth, and killing my husband, I've considered myself a rather pathetic human. Fear has riddled me. And now that I'm wiser, I see that fear is useful for life-or-death decisions, but it hinders daily life. If fear is how you cruise through life, it's not living—it's merely surviving. If you remain a victim and don't take control of your life, nobody will do it for you.

Unless you wish to be controlled.

But look at me now. Jail isn't a pleasant place to be, but it taught me valuable lessons. It's weird to say this, but I'm truly grateful for the experience.

I snap out of my thoughts when I see Andrew walking in my direction, shielding his face from the glare of the sun, and smiling. I watch him trudge through the sand. He's approaching sixty-five, but he's in great shape and looks much younger. He's been single for nearly a decade, and I can't help but wonder why, as I watch him power across the beach. Apparently, his wife cheated on him with his best buddy, which led to a divorce. Without delay, he cut off all communication with his supposed "best" buddy, resulting in his circle disintegrating rapidly. At least he's close to his younger sister, whom I haven't met yet. She lives two towns over, and she's some kind of educator, that's all I know. I will meet her in due time, Andrew recently informed me.

He said he'd been devastated when he found out about his wife's affair and his best friend's disloyalty, but he was over it now. No reason to dwell on the pain for too long. He may be single now, but my gut tells me that will soon change.

"Hey." He sits next to me and taps me on my right hand.

"Hi." I remove my sunglasses as I greet him. "Thanks for stopping by. I hope I didn't take you away from anything."

"Oh, no." He shakes his head. "I was just relaxing in my yard. I could use company."

Me too.

"I went to visit my old neighborhood earlier." I clear my throat. "There's a woman we used to live next door. Her name is Rose. She's now quite aged and not looking so good anymore."

Andrew's gaze intensifies as he listens.

"Well, I asked her about Lucy, and she told me she came to visit a few times over the past few months. I got excited until she also said that Jimmy came to visit last month, too."

Andrew lets out a chuckle, though he apologizes, but then we both laugh, and it feels good to release some of the pent-up tension.

The laughter halts, and I continue. "I feel bad for her, but she's lost it. Poor thing."

"Sounds like it," Andrew says.

A couple with two children walk by, and we sit and watch them in silence, as if lost on what to do next.

Then an idea sparks in my head. How did I not think of it before?

"I just remembered something." My voice comes out high-pitched from excitement. "Jimmy has two other children besides Lucy. I wonder if Lucy might have gotten in touch with them at all? Or maybe they know about her whereabouts. Do you think you can look into it?"

Andrew looks at me, puzzled. "Two other children?"

"Yeah." I divert my eyes in shame, as I reflect on all the

things I've allowed Jimmy to do in our marriage. From extramarital affairs to all the abuse. What the hell was wrong with me? I continue, "I didn't learn about them until I won the lottery, and our names got plastered all over the news."

"That's usually the case. It's interesting to see how people come out of the woodwork when money is in the picture."

"For better or for worse."

"What are their names?" Andrew is already on it, pulling his notebook out of his pocket.

"Cheryl and Emma. And as far as I remember, they still have Jimmy's last name. Corrigan."

"Got it. I'll look into it soon."

I drop my head down, suddenly overwhelmed by the emotions swirling inside me. I was content earlier, but I'm reminded again this is not the life I've wanted to live: half spent with the abusive husband, some of it in the jail, and now chasing my birth daughter. I just want to spend the last years of my life content and peaceful.

Andrew can tell something is wrong. "Are you okay, Lynn?"

He leans toward me, so his eyes can meet mine. I look at him shyly as a tear forms in the corner of my eye.

"Are you crying?"

He takes my hand and cradles it.

I nod and sniffle and wipe my nose with my hand.

"Hey, listen, everything will be fine. Don't worry. I'm here for you, okay? Everything will be fine."

I don't know what *fine* even means anymore, but I still find comfort in Andrew's words.

He caresses my hand and looks at me with his big, warm eyes. He pulls me closer, placing his hand on the back of my head. It's been so long since I felt someone's warmth. It feels paralyzing, but so, so good.

After a few moments, he releases me from his hug, looks at me, and smiles. "Lynn, I like you, and I'll do everything to make you happy."

My heart swells at his next confession.

"I've liked you—really liked you—since the moment we met." He blushes and looks away. "That wasn't the only reason I wanted to help you. I knew your were innocent, but there's more to it than that. Like I said, I'd do anything for you."

CHAPTER 13

AFTER LEAVING THE BEACH, we go back to my place, and Andrew and I spend all night talking.

The spark between us has grown into a fire, and it isn't letting up.

Now it's all become clear as to why he visited me in jail, or wants to help so desperately, or doesn't want to charge me for his services. Having become a better judge of character, based on my jail experience, I fully trust him.

And I like him.

Very much so, even though I pinch myself into admission. We have both been broken, but a new aura of hope has followed us back from the beach. Andrew makes me feel good, and that's a good enough reason for me not to question his motive.

I mean, look, he's starting a relationship with a former convict and murderer. He has passed the test in my books.

But now he's told me he always believed I was innocent. And that I was good, deep down. Just misguided in life.

After cuddling up with him on the couch with a Chinese takeout, I can feel the joy pulsing through my veins. Is this what a healthy relationship looks like? When a man listens and doesn't belittle you, and doesn't punish you for having different thoughts from him?

In the morning, I wake with a throbbing head, even though there's not one reason it should be. I didn't even drink any alcohol. I look around, disoriented, as if I'm dreaming. I expect to see metal bars and a toilet in the corner, and a guard approaching to take me to the kitchen, but none of it materializes, and I let out a deep sigh of relief.

Then I hear a commotion in the kitchen.

The memory of talking to Andrew all night comes to the forefront of my mind, and somehow, the headache becomes less of a concern. I smile. Part of me is afraid that what Andrew and I are building is just an illusion. Because all my life, I've known only the bad and the ugly. Now that the good is being introduced, I need to learn to get used to it, to accept it. Because we all deserve the good in life, don't we?

I trudge to the kitchen and find Andrew making coffee and breakfast. I smell bacon and eggs and freshly squeezed orange juice. He sees me and squares his body toward me. "Good morning, sunshine."

"Hey, look at you, Chef Andrew." I laugh. "You're finally putting those hidden talents to the test, I see."

"Well, I've been waiting for ten years. I'm glad I can do it for the right gal." He winks at me and smiles, then continues to prepare food.

What a difference between him and Jimmy. Like life and death—literally.

We eat breakfast at the kitchen island, and Andrew reminds me he's going to start looking for Emma and Cheryl today. He hopes they'll be easier to locate and, when found, one of them would know about Lucy's whereabouts.

"And what are your plans today, young lady?" Andrew asks playfully.

I take a bite of bacon and chew it slowly while composing my thoughts. I don't want to alarm Andrew about my upcoming plans, but I decide to disclose them fully.

"I have one more person to visit, and I will do it this afternoon."

His brows stitch together from curiosity, and he stops chewing, awaiting the news. I think he's more concerned about me than anything. "Like who?"

"Remember the guy who called the cops on me? Skull. I'm paying him a visit today."

He places the remaining piece of bacon on the plate and wipes his mouth with the napkin from his lap. Maybe he's not so sure this is a good idea. But I have no choice but to confront Skull, eventually.

"Want me to come?"

I shake my head. "No, no. I don't think it's necessary. But thank you."

He widens his eyes as he speaks. "Are you sure?"

"Positive." I smile to reassure him.

"I don't want anything to happen to you, Lynn."

If anything is to happen to me? Everything has *already* happened. It can't get any worse.

"I'll call if I need you."

"You do that."

He gets up and plants a gentle kiss on my cheek. I feel butterflies in my stomach. And happiness. I can't tell you how long it's been since I felt that way.

CHAPTER 14

LATER THAT AFTERNOON, I head to Skull's place.

I'm not sure if he still lives in that big house on the periphery of town, but if the internet is to be trusted, he does. I drive down the pebbly road leading to his house, remembering that dreadful day when I came to see him and begged him not to go to the police. I shake my head to dislodge the memories. They won't do me any good today.

I park by a tree, which has grown very tall in the past five years. I look around to check for any signs of Skull. The bushes by the fence are looking overgrown and neglected. If I remember correctly, the last time I was here, his garden was immaculate, adorned with beautiful flowers. Nothing of that nature today. Maybe Skull doesn't live here after all? Or?

His car isn't parked in the front, and the house appears to be empty, so I am assuming he's not home. I lean against my seat and turn on the radio for some music. And I wait. I have nothing else to do with my time, and this is important, so patience and persistency are key.

Just as Elton John's "I'm Still Standing," my favorite song in the whole wide world plays, a car reemerges from the corner. I'm peeved, because it disrupts my song, but relieved because Skull is here, and I will have a chance to talk to him.

The car stops by the front door, and the figure stays inside longer than I want him to.

Is that Skull or someone else?

The car door opens, and a middle-aged man appears. *Skull.*

My eyes widen in surprise. My goodness—he has changed. The muscles that once used to be a part of his signature look, have turned into an ugly mass. A big pouch protrudes from his belly, and wrinkles sport his face.

He sees my car and does a double take, then comes to a sharp stop. I see the fear in his eyes as his lips tremble. What has happened to Skull?

I climb out of my car and slowly walk to Skull. I don't want to scare him even more, so I wave at him and say hello, so he can relax and recognize my voice. Or at least as relaxed as you can be to face someone whose life you've once ruined.

"Lynn?" Hs eyes are wide. "Lynn, is that you?"

Now I'm only a few feet away from Skull. With a calm voice, I say, "Hey, Skull. Or should I say Evan?" I smile.

"Whatever works." His fear is replaced with relief. He

surveys me up and down, then adds, "Wow, Lynn. You look incredible."

I wish I could say "you too," but I just can't bring myself to lie. "Thanks."

"Do you want to come in?"

"I do, Skull. You know I was dying to see you."

"Yeah?"

I'm surprised he's acting like nothing happened five years ago. Like he never ratted me out and went to the police to report Jimmy's murder. We are not friends, and I hope to make that clear today.

We walk through the front door and find ourselves in the open concept house with tall ceilings adorned with wooden beams across. The furniture smells new. I notice the same pictures of his son sitting by the TV set, those two sad piercing eyes. I wonder if Skull ever reconnected with him.

"Can I get you something to drink?" Skull asks as he places his car keys on the coffee table in the living room.

"Sure. Can I have a vanilla latte with cinnamon and just a tad of sugar?" I pause. "Oh, oh. And if you can keep the foam to a minimum, that will be great."

Skull's shoulders slump and he looks at me defeated, "I ... I don't have that."

I wave my hand at him. "I'm just messing with you."

"Phew." He relaxes.

I'm kind of enjoying making him nervous. "How have you been, Skull?"

He shrugs. "Okay. Can't really complain."

Like me, Skull ended up serving time in jail, but not for as long as me. Unlike me, Skull looks like shit, whereas I am all muscle and invigorated. It's interesting how similar experiences shape people differently.

"How was jail?"

He scoffs. "Do we have to talk about it?"

I nod. "We do, Skull. As a matter of fact, we do. And other things, too."

He cocks his head and looks at me curiously. "Like what?"

I take a deep breath to prepare for what I came here for.

Closure.

I still want to understand why Skull did what he did. Killing Jimmy could have been our secret, and we could have avoided jail time and lived in freedom all those years.

"Like, remember calling the police on me, Skull?" My teeth grind as I speak. "I need to know why you did it."

Skull sighs and makes a sad face. "It was the right thing to do, Lynn."

I stiffen. "Right? By whose definition?"

"Mine. Anyone's with the right conscience. I never should have agreed to be the accessory to murder and dispose of Jimmy's body. And I know you paid me to keep my mouth shut, but let me tell you—fuck money. Ever since I dumped those duffle bags into the ocean, I kept having nightmares. Jimmy was haunting me in my dreams."

I scrutinize his body language, and I sense he's telling

me the truth. But a flicker of doubt creeps in, and I can't but wonder about something else. "It has nothing to do with you having a crush on my daughter, Lucy? I learned you two were quite an item."

Skull gazes down at the floor, then looks at me. "Maybe. At the time. Sure. I did love your daughter and wanted to be with her, even though she'd made it clear it would never happen between us."

"Surprise, surprise!" I shake my head. "You really were smitten by her, weren't you?"

"Besides the point," Skull offers. Then his tone suddenly changes. "Whether or not I liked your daughter, you were planning to kill her, Lynn. Remember? You suggested pushing her off the cliff and making it look like an accident. I know people do all sorts of shit out of fear and paranoia and self-perseverance, but I couldn't let you kill your own daughter, for Christ's sakes, Lynn."

My heart sinks for a moment. It's amazing what a good memory Skull has.

I nod. "Yes, you're right, Skull. I was in the wrong. I shouldn't have suggested I kill my daughter."

He clicks his tongue and points his index finger at me. "You see?"

"I was fucked up, I admit it. But with my current state of mind, I would do things differently. I was just out of my mind with fear back then, I admit it." I shake my head.

"Sure." Skull nods, seemingly uninterested in what I am professing.

"Have you seen her lately?"

Skull shakes his head. "No. She came to jail once, and I never saw her again."

I bite my lip in jealousy: she visited Skull in jail, and not her own mother? My feelings about her are firming up more and more.

"Did she try to get in touch with you, or vice versa, since you've been out of jail?"

"No." He shakes his head slowly.

"You're better off, since you don't know Lucy as well you might think. She's ... sly. Very sly, Skull. And yes, she's my daughter, but she can't be trusted."

"Why?"

"I recently discovered that she witnessed Jimmy tampering with my car brakes. He really did that in an attempt to kill me, and Lucy really did know about it. But she never told me. She pretended like she didn't know all those months."

Skull stares at me with his gigantic eyes and says nothing.

My head starts to spin. "You knew, didn't you, Skull? Did she tell you?" I squint my eyes as I fume inside.

He remains quiet and gazes downward, shaking his head.

"Damn it, Skull. So, you knew, too?"

"She told me when I was in jail." He shrugs. "Not much I could do with the information."

I feel completely disgusted by Lucy. It's almost as if she was going around boasting that she knew about Jimmy trying to kill me.

"Well, my private investigator found the evidence of Jimmy messing with my car. That's why I got out of jail early, in case you wondered. Plus, for good behavior."

"Good for you." Skull oozes sarcasm. "In my defense, though, you wanted your daughter gone before you discovered what she knew."

Skull has a point. I guess he saved me from being charged for double murder, so maybe he's not entirely wrong.

"Lynn, look at me. I've vowed not to hurt people anymore. Calling the cops was the right thing to do, and I'm sorry if that meant you served time in jail." He looks as if he's about to cry.

"It's alright, Skull. I get it."

"Thank you," he musters.

"How's your son? Have you seen him at all?"

"No." His lips curve downward and his eyes droop. Tears form in his eyes.

"You haven't seen him at all?" For some reason, I find myself surprised and shaken by this.

He wipes his face and shakes his head. In a trembling voice, he says, "He doesn't want to see me. I've lost him forever."

He stifles a sob.

I'm anchored to my spot as I watch Skull unleash his sadness. I think I know how he feels. Or, at least, I try to.

Skull has been fighting his demons for so many years. I don't need to add to his pain. In that moment, something inside me snaps and compels me to do something extraordinary.

I decide to forgive him. It's the right thing to do. Forgiving Skull doesn't mean we will resume our friendship and live happily ever after. It just means I can move on from it and live my life the best I can with clear conscience.

I approach him and give him a brief hug. "Take care of yourself, Skull."

He squeezes me hard for a few seconds, then lets me go.

"I wish you all the best, Lynn."

With that, I head out the door and never look back.

CHAPTER 15

MY VISIT with Skull concluded my relationship with him.

The meeting didn't go as I envisioned, but I still got my closure. Forgiveness is the right thing to do. Forgiveness is one of those things that is not intuitive. You have to work hard at it, but once you do, a big burden falls off you. It's easier to move on.

I'll probably never see him again unless we stumble upon each other, a high possibility in this small town. But I hope not.

I drive down the main road by the beach, which is full of people, mostly tourists. It's a slow ride, because I have to stop at every crosswalk to let people walk by. I'm usually impatient and cuss under my breath when I see people slogging across the street, like they don't have a care in the world.

But today, I don't mind.

Today, I give a closer look at everyone, especially women. I check for their frames and faces, wondering if any resemble Lucy's. It's been five years since I last saw her in that stuffy courtroom, so it's possible my memory of her has gotten distorted in my mind. Do I remember her as well as I believe I do?

Maybe she's gained weight since and cut her hair short or colored it blonde. Maybe she's wearing glasses, making her look more serious. Maybe her body is covered in ever-growing tattoos, making it impossible to recognize her.

None of these women are Lucy.

While I'm out and about, I feel the pull toward my house and the urge to drive by it. I'm curious what Charlotte might be up to. I'm dying to get to know her better. I feel like I was her at one point, caught in the claws of a spouse who likes to control and have the last word in. Maybe I can help her, whatever that might entail.

When I arrive, the street is silent. The cul-de-sac has always been mysterious, but today, it's so quiet that it sends shivers down my spine. It's a gorgeous sunny day, so I'd expect Charlotte's kids to be playing in the pool and acting rambunctious like the last time we saw them.

Which was two days ago.

I park in front of the house, and I get a nauseating feeling that something is wrong. I clutch my phone, immediately thinking of calling Andrew, but something sitting on the gate catches my eye.

I lean forward to get a better look. A white envelope is taped between the two gate bars, glowing in the sun.

Curiosity gets the better of me. I get out of the car and

look beyond the gate to check for any movements in or around the house. Nothing.

I approach the gate and flinch when I see my name scribbled on the envelope:

FOR LYNN MILLER

I un-tape it slowly and flip the envelope back and forth, testing its contents. It feels light. Should I open it now, or should I wait to get home and open in front of Andrew?

I shake my head. Every inch inside me is eager to delve in.

I run to my car and sit at the steering wheel, turning up the AC to the max. That air blowing in my face feels good, especially as I'm feeling so dizzy.

When I open the envelope, there's a piece of paper holding what appears to be a personal note from the family.

Lynn,

It was nice to meet you the other day.

After careful consideration, we decided to move out sooner than we originally planned. Our new home in Texas is ready, and frankly, we are eager to get settled down as soon as possible.

We apologize for not telling you in a different manner, but after you left, we realized we didn't exchange phone numbers, and we had no way of reaching you.

We enjoyed living in your beautiful home and wish you many more beautiful memories in it once you move. The house is in the same condition as we found it.

Best regards,
Gabriel and Charlotte (and the kids)

I read it again, in case I might have missed an important detail, but it seems as clear as day: they are gone, and the house is all mine. The gate is unlocked, and I trudge through carefully.

The front yard is peaceful, though the pool is looking sad without the kids having fun in it. The French doors to the kitchen feels like a portal, like a door back to my past, but I ascend the steps and open them, finding myself in awe of the house all over again. It's almost hard to believe it's all mine.

I look around, and everything seems perfectly fine. Walking around the house, I ensure that no traces of the family are left behind. The house is habitable, and I could move back in today if I wanted to. I'll just need to change the key lock to the gate and front doors, just to be safe.

I sit on the couch and let out an enormous sigh of relief. I realize I am still holding the note from Gabriel and Charlotte, and I look at it again, unsettled by their quick departure.

As I flip the page, I notice another note at the very bottom. It looks like it's been written by someone other than the person who wrote the main note.

My eyes are drawn to the urgent scrawl.

She's not who you think she is.

. . .

I flip the page back and forth as if to shake out this latest surprise so I can hold it in my hands and examine it from every angle.

What does it mean? Who wrote it? Could Charlotte possibly be trying to send me an important message covertly?

I imagine her sneaking the note in before the envelope was sealed.

If she did, who is "she?" Maybe Suzanne?

I might never find out, but my gut feeling tells me it might be her. Another puzzle to solve, I guess.

A text from Andrew comes through:

> Lynn, call me ASAP. I've got info on Jimmy's daughters.

CHAPTER 16

I DIAL ANDREW RIGHT AWAY.

"Hey, you're never going to believe this," Andrew says.

"I could say the same," I quip.

"Why? What happened?"

"I stopped by my house just to briefly inspect it, and guess what?"

"What?" Andrew's voice brims with anticipation.

"The family has moved out already. They're gone."

"Seriously?"

"Seriously. As a matter of fact, I'm sitting on the couch in my living room. And it's kind of creepy, actually." I look around, as if expecting to see a ghost.

There's brief silence until Andrew says. "Stay put. I'll be right there."

A smile crosses my lips. Andrew being next to me comforts me.

"Okay. I'll see you soon."

We hang up, and I head to the kitchen to get myself a

drink. I hope the family has left something delicious I can quench my thirst with. I open the fridge and don't see anything but half a carton of milk. I crunch my nose. I'm not in the mood for milk.

I shut the fridge door and do a double take when I notice a card sitting on the edge, propped by a magnet from the town trash collector. I cock my head, study it and wonder what it is.

I remove the magnet and take the card in my hands. The front is pretty, but somewhat faded, with a beautiful house surrounded by flowers and a message across it: WELCOME HOME.

This should be interesting. The family took every-thing, except for this note. My guess is that they either forgot it or didn't care for it. Either way, I'm curious to find out what's inside.

I open it and read a note:

Welcome to your new abode! I was happy to serve your real estate needs. Make yourselves comfortable.
   Claire

My head snaps in surprise. Who on earth is Claire now? I thought Gabriel said it was someone called Suzanne who rented out my house?

Out of frustration, I flick the note into the air, and it lands on the floor next to the kitchen island. I don't know what to make of this.

And now Claire? Andrew will at least have more to work with. And hopefully, he will be successful.

Half an hour later, Andrew arrives. He has seen the outside of the house, but not the inside. As he walks around, he lets out periodic awestruck whistles every time he sees something that highly impresses him.

"Wow."

I let him take a tour on his own, so he goes upstairs and wanders through the bedrooms and bathrooms.

Ten minutes later, he descends the stairs and smiles at me. "You've got quite a place here, missy. You could fit an entire army here."

"I know." I laugh. I appreciate Andrew's sense of humor and lightness. He makes me forget the shitty life I'd had. Spending time with him almost makes me want to give up on searching for Lucy, but he keeps reminding me I would be better off finding her and getting closure.

We sit at the kitchen island across from each other, and I cross my arms, awaiting to hear Andrew's discovery.

"And?"

He shakes his head. "Not good."

I widen my eyes. "Not good? Again? How not good this time? You're making me nervous now."

"I got the info on his daughters, Emma and Cheryl." He pauses. "Unfortunately, that door is closed."

"What do you mean?"

He glances away and pales a little. "Both Cheryl and Emma are dead."

My stomach plummets. "I'm sorry. What?"

Andrew nods. "Yeah, they're both dead. Gone. I found their obituaries. They died a couple of years within each other."

"How?"

My mind goes wild. Did Lucy have anything to do with their deaths? Probably a weird thought to jump to, but maybe I'm just so peeved at her that I'm accusing her of the unimaginable.

"Emma died in a car crash."

I gasp as I recall my car accident that nearly sent me to death.

"A car crash? That sounds like a strange coincidence," I point out.

"Actually, no. It was DUI. Her car was spotted on Route 93 by a police trooper. It was flipped upside down, sitting on the shoulder. He found her lifeless body inside."

I bring my hand to my mouth and widen my eyes. "Dear lord. How old was she?"

"She'd just turned twenty-one. Apparently, she went out to celebrate her birthday and got really drunk. Lost control of her wheel and smashed into a tree. Instantly dead."

"Poor thing." We let the silence settle between us as we stare at each other. "What about Cheryl?" I finally muster the strength to speak up.

"Cheryl died of some rare disease. I couldn't find any information about what kind of disease." He shrugs his shoulders. "But I suppose it doesn't matter."

"I guess not." It's crazy to think that Jimmy's other daughters are both dead. His lineage is nearly gone. I can't help but wonder yet again what has happened to Lucy and where she is.

"I know this is a lot of information to take all in," Andrew says. "Maybe I can cheer you up and take you out to dinner. What do you say?" He looks at me with puppy eyes, as if hoping I will say yes. It's not such a bad idea. I need to take my mind off this news.

"Okay."

"Great," he says.

He stands up and goes to the kitchen, and as he gets closer, his steps halt. He bends down and grabs the card from the floor. I watch him read it with the intensity of someone reading *Inferno* by Dante.

He looks at me, and his voice rises in pitch. "Claire? Who on earth is Claire?"

CHAPTER 17

THE FOLLOWING DAY, I move into the mansion. Why wait?

The temporary apartment was comfortable, but I'd rather prefer to enjoy ocean views from a short distance. It doesn't take long to get used to it. I sit by the pool to soak up the sun and watch the boats bob on the water in a distance. It's awfully quiet. I wish I had friends to invite over, but everyone had given up on me or moved away in the past five years.

By the evening, however, once the darkness has enveloped the town, and the ocean looks like a giant dark background, the vibe of the house turns creepy. I walk into the kitchen and pause, listening for any sounds. The eerie quiet makes the place seem even creepier.

An unsettling feeling of foreboding follows me around. I feel as if someone or something is constantly watching me. Or is it the memories attached to the place that keep lingering in my mind?

I remember the day Lucy and I moved in here. It was truly one of the happiest days ever. We were all giddy as we explored the space in disbelief that all this belonged to us. Lucy seemed so innocent and happy. She presented me with a photo album filled with pictures from her childhood. She'd beamed with joy, wanting me to be a part of it.

In another distant memory, I was riddled with fear, and I simply couldn't focus on her joy. And how could I if Jimmy's murder was all that was on my mind?

The early memories play like a movie in my head, and they slip to the housewarming party. That was an ordeal. No one suspected I'd murdered Jimmy, even though I was clearly a ball of nerves. It was easy to fool people and make them believe we were getting a divorce. They must have thought—*finally, she's seen sense.* Lucy's friends had been eyeing me strangely, though, and I noticed them roll their eyes at me. My guess is none of them liked me.

And my old boss, Barbara? She knew that Skull and Lucy knew each other, but she pretended she didn't. That just tells you where her loyalty was. To her defense, she'd known Skull a lot longer than me.

As my mind shuffles through the list of people who came to the party, something occurs to me. It's not just the people who came, but it's also those who didn't.

Lucy's stepfather, Fred.

He couldn't make it to the party, because the weather in North Carolina prevented the plane from taking off.

Oh my God, what am I thinking?

A bolt of energy courses through me as I think of my next step.

I take out my phone and locate Fred's phone number. I hope he hasn't changed it. But why do I have his phone number? Lucy was secretive from the very beginning, so there had to be a reason.

Then I remember. Lucy didn't give me his phone number. I stole it from her phone when she went to the bathroom once. Fred was always an enigma, and I was hoping I would put his phone number to use. Who knew it would come in handy someday?

I'm a little shaky but determined to call him. He's got to know Lucy's whereabouts, surely? If he doesn't, all hope is lost, and I'm clueless about how to trace her. But I won't know until I try.

I dial, and the phone rings. At the second ring, a disoriented male voice answers.

I clear my throat. "Is this Fred?"

"Speaking." Pause. "Who is this?"

"This is Lynn," I say.

"Lynn who?"

I want to introduce myself as Lucy's mother, but I change my mind. I don't want him to be guarded right away. "Lynn Miller," I say instead.

Dead silence on the other side of the line. Did I rattle his cage?

"Hello? Are you there?" I look at my phone to make sure I'm still connected.

"Yes, sorry. I had to think about who Lynn Miller is. You're Lucy's mother, correct?"

I sigh in relief. "Yes, that's me."

"Great to hear from you," he says. Not what I expect to hear.

"Thank you for taking my call," I say. "As you know, I was in prison for a while, but I just came out." I realize the words are rushing out at full pelt and sound unnaturally high-pitched. I slow down. "Thankfully, more evidence surfaced that proved me innocent."

"Well, that's good." He keeps his voice even.

"Here's the thing, though. Ever since I came out, I haven't been able to locate Lucy. It's as if she has fallen from the face of the Earth. So, I'm hoping you can help me connect me with her? I really need to talk to her."

I'm afraid I sound too whiny, but maybe that's the effect I should go for. A mother desperate to talk to her child. Who wouldn't empathize with that?

However, there's silence on the other side again. I hear some background noise, but I cannot discern what it is. Fred's breathing comes into the foreground, and it's making me anxious. He's not saying a word.

Is he preparing a perfect response to tell me she is missing or dead, or whichever other catastrophe could happen to a human? My stomach churns.

"Fred? What is it? Did something happen to Lucy?"

"No. No." His voice has changed. And he doesn't sound convincing. "Well, since you are her mother, I guess I can tell you that Lucy and I no longer talk."

I gasp. How is this possible? Lucy was always close to her stepfather. She spoke of him fondly all the time and swore by his love.

"Why? What happened?"

"Well, let me just tell you, Lynn." His voice perks up a bit. "Lucy is not the person I raised and loved. She ... she has changed so much to the point of being unrecognizable."

It's my turn to be quiet. A somber silence lingers between us, and neither of us says a word for long seconds.

"I'm sorry, Lynn. I wish I had better news for you."

"Can you at least give me her latest phone number? I really need to reach her." Here I am, sounding whiny again.

"Yeah ... that ... Lucy and I haven't spoken for over a year. The phone number I have for her is disconnected."

"So, you've lost all your connection to her?"

"I'm afraid so." Not an ounce of regret stems from his voice.

I chew my lip. "What about her email address?"

"Email address? People still use email?" he scoffs. A distant voice in the background calls his name. "Hey, listen, I gotta go now, but it was nice talking to you, and good luck with everything."

The phone goes dead.

A rush of unease takes over me.

The room spins as I clutch the edge of the table, my breath coming in shallow gasps. My heart races, pounding erratically against my ribs. A cold sweat breaks out on my forehead, and my vision blurs. My legs tremble, feeling like jelly beneath me, unable to support my weight. I try to steady myself, but the ground sways, a nauseating tilt that sends my stomach churning. A roar of blood rushes in my ears. My knees buckle, and I descend into darkness, consumed by the overwhelming tide of anxiety.

CHAPTER 18

THE BRIGHTNESS OUTSIDE makes my eyes squint.

I lift my head with difficulty and notice I'm stretched on the couch in my living room. I don't remember how I got here. Why was I sleeping on the couch and not in my bed last night? I can vaguely recall losing consciousness and falling, but what happened next is a complete blank. I check parts of my body for any injuries, and I'm relieved when I find none. The fall couldn't have been bad.

I peek at the clock on the wall, and it shows seven in the morning. It's the usual time I wake up every day, but something is different today. I can't point my finger.

A clattering in the kitchen causes me to crane my neck. I see no one. Instant fear kicks in, and I retreat onto the couch, listening. Did someone break in? I don't know why, but Lucy comes to mind first. Has she returned? Did she find out that I got out of jail, and come back for a second chance?

I listen carefully, hoping any slight movements will

reveal the intruder. A little hum, a cuss word under their breath ... anything. But all I hear is the mugs or plates moved from one place to another.

Who is this?

Surprise replaces fear when Andrew walks across the living room. The tension inside me releases instantly as our eyes meet. My shoulders slump and I roll my eyes involuntarily. "What are you doing here? You scared the crap out of me."

He stops in the middle of the living room. "Hey, you're awake." He gazes at the doors. "You left all your doors unlocked, young lady. Don't you think you should lock doors at night?"

"I must have forgotten." I rub my head, still feeling cloudy. "When did you get here?"

"This morning. I found you lying on the floor next to the coffee table. If I may suggest, a couch or a bed is a lot more comfortable." He smiles.

"Ha, ha." I quip. "You really think I wanted to sleep on the floor last night?"

Andrew looks at me, puzzled, and cocks his head. "What? You didn't?"

"No, silly! I think I lost consciousness and fell to the floor last night." I shrug. "No idea what happened."

Andrew sits next to me and takes my hand. "Are you okay now? Can I get you anything?"

"Maybe a glass of water. Thank you."

Andrew gets up and trots to the kitchen. "Maybe you

should go see a doctor and get some blood tests!" he yells across the floor, so I can hear his advice.

Doctors. Like the one who falsely diagnosed me with lung cancer? I don't trust doctors, and besides, I feel physically okay. It was anxiety that got me all worked up last night.

He returns with a glass of iced water and something else in his hand. A cracker.

"Take this, too. You're probably starved, right?"

"I could eat."

Only then do I feel my stomach reacting in protest. I'm hungry for sure.

"Okay, let me make something real quick."

Before he goes to the kitchen, I ask, "So, what brings you here this early in the morning?" I trust Andrew wholeheartedly, but I still question some of his actions. Like coming to my place unannounced.

"I called you several times last night, and I didn't hear from you. I thought you'd probably fallen asleep. But when I called you again this morning, you didn't answer your phone, and that's when I headed over to your place. It was all unlocked. You really should be more careful."

I frown. "Why did you call me?"

"Just to give you updates on my search progress. I've been banging my head against the wall, and I have found nothing on Lucy yet. I barely slept last night, thinking about where else to look."

I tell him about calling Fred and what he said about Lucy.

"Wow. Lucy's changed how?" Andrew asked with a fascinated frown.

"I didn't ask the specifics. But it can't be good if they don't talk anymore."

Andrew goes to the kitchen to prepare whatever food I have—not much. But knowing Andrew and his creative juices, he'll come up with something.

I lie back down and relax. I'll let Andrew take care of me. For once, there's a man in my life who cares about my well-being.

My eyes dart around the room, and I notice the intricate details on the ceiling. The crown moldings. As they come into greater focus, their forms begin to swirl and distort, their invisible arms extending toward me and trying to choke me. I close my eyes and whisper, "Go away" through my clenched teeth, but when I open my eyes, the invisible hands are still there. They're about to clutch my neck and strangle me.

I shake my head and prop myself up in fear. I really don't want to scream and draw attention to myself unnecessarily. Andrew would jump to my rescue immediately, but I don't want him to worry about me. I know it's just a weird image playing in my head, trying to trick me into believing ghosts are haunting me.

In the pit of my stomach, I feel nauseated. I haven't felt sick like this in a long time, but I suddenly understand what the culprit is.

It's this damned house.

I nod to myself as I agree on the next step. It's the only way to escape the past, the only way to fight the demons.

Andrew steps into the living room to call for me. The breakfast is ready. But I'm rooted to my spot and can't move.

"Andrew?"

"Yes, dear?"

Then I announce, "I need to get out of this house as soon as possible. I'm going to put it up for sale today."

CHAPTER 19

WE SIT at the kitchen table and eat whatever Andrew has prepared for breakfast. Toast with butter and marmalade, and coffee.

"Are you sure you want to put it up for sale?" Andrew asks.

I nod as the scary images of the hands flash in front of my eyes. "Yes. Besides, the house is too big. I can stay in my rented apartment until I sell the place and get something else. It definitely won't be as big as this one."

Andrew pauses for a second and fidgets in his seat. He looks nervous, and I can tell he has something on mind.

"What is it, Andrew?" My voice is gentle.

"I was thinking ..." He puts his toast on the plate and gazes down at the table. He looks up and says, "First, I want to say, in case you didn't know, I like you a lot, Lynn." His eyes glisten as he speaks.

"And I know we're still getting to know each other, but I've known you for over five years now. And I care about you a lot. Probably even more than I confessed to you the other day." He cocks his head and creases his brows.

I freeze as he professes his feelings to me. I like Andrew, too. But my disastrous marriage has taught me to be guarded and distant and careful. But here's the thing: I've read so many romance and dating self-help books in jail that I've learned what a healthy relationship looks like. It's built on trust and respect. Acceptance and love are cousins of those, and that's what sustains a healthy couple. Besides, I like Andrew. It's been a while since I felt comfortable with someone's presence all the time.

I smile. I know I can have all of this with Andrew, and I trust him with all my heart.

"I know it's early in our relationship, but I was wondering if, when your lease expires, you would want to move in with me?" He doesn't let me chime in and rushes to say, "It's okay, you don't have to answer now, and you can think about it. And I totally understand if you say no."

Another thing I've learned from the books is that men have a harder time staying single than women do. They often need companionship, someone to grow old with. Andrew has told me frequently he was ready for a relation-ship. I guess we're together, anyway. We trust and respect each other.

"Andrew, you're so sweet," I say.

"So are you, Lynn." He gently takes my hand. "You make me happy."

Overwhelmed, I remove my hand and feel tears well up in my eyes. It's been a while since I cried. But I think these are happy tears. I wipe them at once and turn around. "Well, I think I'm going to be busy today. I need to call my real estate agent, Cecilia."

"Okay." Andrew stands up and comes close. He hugs me and looks me in the eye. "Think about it, okay?"

I nod, "Sure." Although, in my mind, I've already decided.

———

I dial Cecilia, and she answers the phone right away. At least she's still around. And with the same phone number.

I introduce myself, and she appears to remember me immediately. "Lynn Miller? Of course I remember you! How could I forget you?"

I'm not sure this is good or bad, but I am grateful I don't need to explain who I am.

"I sold you that big house on Ocean Boulevard a few years back. How's it going?"

I fully expected Cecilia to mention something about me killing Jimmy, but she doesn't. Maybe she's just being diplomatic, but I still find relief in avoiding the subject. I continue, "Well, that's the reason I'm calling. I'd like to put it on the market."

Cecilia doesn't seem to be fazed by the news. "No problem. I can help you with all your real estate needs. Do you have time to meet and go over some details? I also need you to sign some paperwork. Just a formality."

"No problem."

In all honesty, I'd just about give my left pinky for help to get rid of the house. We agree to meet in her office at noon and go from there.

I take one last tour before I mentally say goodbye to it. There could have been so many happy memories built in this beautiful place, but luck had it otherwise. When I spend time here, all I think of is my failed relationship with my long-lost daughter, and all the fear I felt when I first moved in here. After this tour, I don't want to come back here ever again unless I absolutely must.

That image I saw this morning ... my goodness, it felt like I was living a horror movie. But I no longer wish to take part in it. Luckily, I don't have many things to move. Only a box or two of personal items. I walk around the house for a last inspection and relief washes over me.

I hope some happy family will buy this house and enjoy it. It's got a lot of potential to become someone's beautiful sanctuary.

I walk out without looking back, sit in my car, and head to see Cecilia. The day is gorgeous. Not too hot like it has been the previous few days. After I meet with Cecilia, my plan is to drive to a secluded little beach a little way from the town and spend some alone time. Think and reflect. Consider my next moves in life.

I think of Andrew and feel lucky. If it wasn't for him, I wouldn't really know what to do with myself. Frankly, I'd be lost.

I arrive at Cecilia's office and find it the same as it had been all those years ago. But Cecilia looks a lot different.

Aging hasn't been kind to her. She's switched her blouses and pencil skirts to wide dresses to accommodate her weight gain. Her face is still bright with a smile, but she has concealed her wrinkles with lots of makeup. If I ran into her on the street, there's no way I would recognize her.

She ushers me into her office and gives me a hug as if we're best friends.

"Lynn, you look amazing." She looks at me up and down.

Second person this week I wish I could say "you too," to but I just can't.

We sit at her oval desk in the middle of the office and exchange small talk. She's shocked when I tell her what has happened to Jimmy.

"Oh, my." Her eyes are wide. "But you know ... I'm not sure I should say this, but I really didn't like the way he treated you the day you two came to my office to discuss the offer on the house. He was ..." she paused, considering her next words, "... kinda mean. It's still quite memorable for me."

"Thank you for saying that." I guess the entire world saw it, except me. Well, not entirely true. I saw it, but my guilt over losing my child led me to believe I deserved his treatment.

Now I know he was just a shithead of a person.

"Let's talk about the house. So, you want to sell it?"

"Yes."

"Okay. Well, since I'm already familiar with it, it shouldn't take long to list it. I'll just need the keys so I can take a look. I'll probably bring a photographer and take fresh photos."

"Excellent. I really appreciate your help, Cecilia." I smile. Things are working as they should. I finally have people by my side who care.

I hand her the key. "Knock yourself out! Take a swim in the pool if you want."

"I just might." She pitches her voice.

"Before I leave, I just have one question for you, Cecilia."

She halts and gives me a concerned frown. "What is it, dear?"

It's probably a long shot, but I decide to test my luck. "Do you happen to know a real estate agent named Claire?"

Cecilia's gaze darts across the ceiling, and her lips move to the side as she's pondering. "Claire, huh? Does she have a last name?"

"Well, that's the thing. I don't have her last name. But apparently, while I was away, she rented my house to a family."

"Oh, my." She places her hand on her chest. "Without your permission?"

"Yep. I'm looking for her, but I cannot find her for the life of me."

"Unfortunately, it doesn't ring a bell with me. But I hope you find her."

Me, too. *Oh, how I'm so desperate to find her.*

We part ways, and I hop in my car to drive to the

secluded beach. The best part of my life right now is that I don't need to rush to be anywhere. Time is on my side.

Halfway in, my phone chimes with a text message. When I drive, I don't look at my phone. I absolutely hate it when people do. Not only do they slow the traffic down, but they could also lose control of their steering wheel and cause a threat to other cars. It's enough I almost died in a car accident once. Anything remotely dangerous sets me off, so I've become extra careful and alert while behind the wheel.

But I'm dying to see who the text is from. Nowadays, I expect them to come from only a few people. Andrew, and maybe now, Cecilia. And by some miracle, perhaps Lucy, who might have searched for me and finally found me.

When I stop at the red light, I snatch my phone and see Andrew's name across the screen. Andrew appears to be becoming a constant presence in my life; texting and calling me and showing up unannounced when I need him the most. I smile, thinking this is his ploy for me to think constantly about him.

But when I open the phone, that feeling quickly dissipates. My blood freezes when I see his message, all in caps.

LYNN, CALL ME IMMEDIATELY. YOU'RE NOT GOING TO BELIEVE WHAT I JUST FOUND OUT.

PART TWO

CHAPTER 20

Claire

THE CAR ENGINE doesn't start even after I turn the key.

"Ugh. Are you kiddin' me?"

It's persistently stubborn, and the engine remains idle. Worst timing. Just when I have to pick up Billy. It wouldn't be so bad if this wasn't my fifth time picking him up late within a month. But I could be on time if only my stupid engine goes on.

I turn the key again. Still nothing. A little light next to the gas tank goes on, and I'm baffled. Apparently, the gas tank is empty, but how is it possible? I refueled my car this morning. To the max.

I don't understand. I jump out of my car to check if the little door of my gas tank is open. Nope. It's tightly shut, and there's nothing suspicious about it.

My body gets into panic mode. I jump back in the car and instinctively reach for my phone. My hands shake, and my mind spins wildly. Who should I call first? My son's daycare or a towing truck? Of course, my son should be my priority, and I should really let his teachers know I'm running late before they kick him out of the program.

The phone rings, and Susan, the daycare director, answers the phone.

"Hi, this is Billy's mom. Mmmm. I am so sorry, but I'm running late. I don't know what happened—"

"Again?"

Susan, a woman in her late fifties, has lectured me a zillion times not to be late. She has told me it is just not good for a kid's psyche when all the other kids leave school with their parents, and they leave him behind, all alone. They feel abandoned and neglected, and that's not something I should make my child feel.

Way to make me feel like the worst mom ever.

Plus, she always reminds me how she will charge me ten dollars for every additional fifteen minutes Billy needs to stay at school beyond six o'clock. The least of my problems right now. The only reason they're as lenient as they are, albeit very annoyed, is that I am a single mom, and I don't have any other human to pick him up when I'm unavailable. Susan should know better, but it's just her shoddy personality that's good at making me feel like shit. Every single time.

"Listen, I'm on my way, but something has happened

to my car. I filled the tank this morning, but the car tells me the tank is empty, and I can't start it."

I know this sounds ridiculous, and Susan probably thinks I'm a nut job. She sighs. "Okay, but hurry. Don't be two hours late like the other day."

I nod quickly several times, even though Susan can't see me. It's my nerves. I want to explain that I was two hours late last time, because my client was late for a house showing. After he'd shown up, we chatted for an hour about the house, because he'd seemed highly interested in it, and I'd lost all sense of time. Before I knew it, I was two hours late.

But Susan doesn't want to hear my excuses. In fact, she'd told me many times she was concerned about my tardiness. Every time I show up at school, she gives me a look of scathing resentment.

I promise to be there as soon as possible and assure her it won't take two hours this time. But I'm on my way— hopefully, that will calm her down.

Next, I dial a tow company and tell them my location. They ask me how I'd ran out of gas, but I tell them what happened. I have no reason to believe this is an accident.

Someone is messing with me.

Someone is trying to turn things against me. It could be a dissatisfied client who I'd promised to sell a house to, but then turned them down when a better offer came along. I wouldn't be the first real estate agent to fall victim to that.

All I know is, this isn't an accident. Someone emptied my gas tank.

But lately, I've been so distracted with everything. Could I have just been dreaming about filling the tank? I trace the steps in my mind from the morning and remember filling the gas tank while holding my morning cup of coffee. But when I think about it more, I start to wonder if that might have happened yesterday or two days ago. Either way, the gas tank shouldn't be empty now. It's not like I've been driving hundreds of miles the past few days.

Wait. But maybe I have.

Until the tow truck finally arrives, I fidget in my seat, counting every passing minute. I've been careful not to piss Susan off, but this was unplanned.

The alternative plan was to take an Uber to the closest gas station, buy gas, and Uber back to my car, but I'm on the major, busy highway and kind of in the middle of nowhere. Cars pass me by, rubbernecking and wondering why I'm sitting on the shoulder of the road. I hide my face, because I don't want people to see me. Plus, I'm ashamed that my son is waiting.

The tow truck gets me to the closest gas station. I look at my watch and see I'm forty-five minutes late. I take a deep breath and close my eyes, reminding myself that I'm close to the finish line.

Once my gas tank is filled, I rush to Billy's school, weaving around other cars, and driving like a maniac. It's not because I'm late, but mainly because I don't want to face and argue with Susan again. She's not someone to reckon with.

Ten minutes later, the sight of the school building releases the tension in my body. I'm here.

When I walk through the door, Susan is sitting at the front desk, her glasses perched on her nose, looking at me with an evil eye. "You've made it." Her voice is cold.

"I'm here," I say in a cheerful voice, but Susan doesn't smile.

"Your son is crying in the classroom." Her voice is stern. Scary. "He's asked about you a million times."

I don't stop to talk to Susan. I walk by the desk and run to the classroom.

I hear a small, whiny voice coming from behind the wall. "When is my mom going to be here?"

"She'll be here soon, sweetheart. How about we read another book?"

That's Billy's teacher, Rebecca. I can sense impatience in her voice, and I don't blame her, since she probably should be home, caring for her own kids.

I step inside the classroom, and they both notice my presence. Rebecca's brows crease and she says nothing as she stands up, ready to leave the room. She walks by me and brushes against my shoulder, not caring enough to apologize.

Billy's still sitting on the floor. His eyes are wide, and his lip is trembling, as if he's about to burst out crying. Unlike other kids I've seen running into their parent's arms, Billy stays put.

We stare at each other until I say, "Let's go, Billy. It's time to go home."

CHAPTER 21

Susan

I CANNOT STAND THIS WOMAN.

I've worked at this daycare for almost twenty years, and I've never seen anything like this before. Her lack of care is obvious and blatant, and my heart aches for Billy.

Claire is the only parent in our school who runs repeatedly late to pick up her child. I could count on two hands the number of times she arrived on time.

I watch her and Billy walking down the hallway, Billy trotting behind her, his gaze fixed downward. She tells him to hurry, which is ironic, since she doesn't seem to care to hurry herself, and opens the door for him. Claire looks at me for a second and says nothing. Billy walks through the door, and they both disappear from my view.

My shoulders slump and I sigh. I'm tired. In my late

fifties, I should be more carefree. Not worrying about children whose parents don't even care.

Before I leave the school for the day, I lock the front door and sit back at my desk to check some registration paperwork. I need to make sure we have everything to ensure the smooth and legal running of the place. We're due for an inspection, and any mishap could lead the school to close for good, and I don't want that to happen.

When I get to Billy's records, my curiosity rises. I lean forward in anticipation to see all his record notes.

Born August 15, 2020. He's just turned three. According to the doctor's notes, he's mostly healthy, but his BMI is under average, according to the CDC data. Speech and cognitive development delayed. Living with mother. Father unknown.

At school, Billy's behavior oscillates between being reserved and shy to being overly stimulated. There's no middle ground for him. The teachers have complained that he's sometimes difficult to handle and that constant watch over him is often needed. He doesn't play with other kids in the classroom. In fact, he approaches them abruptly and bites them sometimes out of the blue.

We have had a talk with Claire about it, but she shrugs her shoulders and says it's just a phase. He doesn't bite at home, and it's our responsibility to ensure it doesn't happen at school. The *nerve* of that woman.

I shake my head in frustration. But there's nothing I can do about it. I have no evidence that she's neglectful or abusive to the child.

It's time to go home. My husband, Scott, texted me an hour ago to let me know dinner was ready. We've been married for thirty years, and he's been nothing but loving and kind. A keeper, that's for sure. He likes to cook, so I consider myself lucky. Being retired already, he has all the time in the world to do chores around the house and prepare dinner. And boy, can he cook!

I double check all the classrooms to make sure no one is lingering. All good.

On my way out, I secure the lock on the door and push it twice to ensure it's locked. It's a habit I've developed over decades.

My car is parked on the other side of the building, because we leave the front lot empty for parents who drop off and pick up their children. The day is beautiful, sunny, not a cloud in the sky. My old Acura is sitting lonesome in the parking lot. I've just remembered—I should pick up a bottle of white wine on my way home. Tonight's dinner is scallops with rice and salad.

When I sit in my car, I almost forget to do something. Something very important. I take my phone out of my purse, open a text message and type:

CHAPTER 22

Claire

ON OUR WAY HOME, I watch Billy's face in the rearview mirror. He's frowning in his car seat, and his arms are crossed over his torso.

"Hey, Billy, you okay?"

His gaze shifts in my direction but doesn't stay long. He's back to looking down, staying quiet. To get him to talk is difficult, and sometimes I get so frustrated by him not responding that I shout at him, forcing him to speak.

I look ahead to concentrate on the road. Lately, Billy hasn't been the only one I worry about. My job stresses me out, too. Being a real estate agent sometimes feels like a thankless career. All I do is chase after clients to secure a commission, but the field is so competitive—there are hundreds of other real estate agents in town, and only so many available properties for sale or rent. Several clients have been close to signing with me exclusively, but all of them backed out after I was late for a meeting or didn't respond to their phone calls on time. They are ruthless. They don't understand what it's like to be a single mother with no husband or family around to help with raising the child.

Not to mention that my checking account is depleting fast. Billy's school costs $2000 a month, but I can't find other, less expensive alternative. He's too young to stay home alone. I wish things weren't as dire as they are.

As I drive, I check my phone to see if I've received any phone calls with new leads. I'm desperate to take on a listing or two. Lately, all I've done is take care of rentals, but the income on those equals less than a monthly payment for Billy's school.

I'm totally screwed. That reminds me, I should check the balance of my checking account and hope it's not as bad as I think it is.

We pull into the driveway of our house, and Billy extends his arm. "Home."

"Yeah, buddy, that's where we live."

Our home is nothing to wow about. It resembles a small cabin, perched in the back of the woods. That's all I can afford for now, though. It's enough for me and my little boy. We share the same bed, and there's another room where Billy spreads his toys around and plays with them. He loves that room, or so I think. He spends a considerable amount of time in there, minding his own business, playing with his toys. Interesting how kids develop personality at an early age. Billy, even at his young age, likes his space.

I exit the car and help him out of his seat. He seems aggravated. "No, no, no."

I stop unbuckling him and cock my head, feeling my forehead crease. "What's the matter, Billy?"

He screams from the top of his lungs, "No! No home! No home!"

"Well, too bad, since you have no other place to be," I say, annoyed, and resume unbuckling him.

Billy does this every day. He can be extremely difficult, but since he can't express himself well, I can only guess what he's really fussing about.

I remove the seat straps and wrangle him out while he continues to scream and make a scene. He slides out of my hands and falls to the ground. Unfazed, he stands up and runs away in the direction of the main street.

I run after him and catch him two hundred feet in. He's pretty fast and furious for a three-year-old. When I grab him, he laughs. He finds running away and being chased amusing.

I kneel to face him, grab his shoulders and give him a little shake. "Don't you ever run away like that? Do you hear me?" Anger fills me, but I do my best to compose myself. I don't want to hurt Billy.

Billy just stares at me and smirks. Seconds later, he lifts his hand and hits me hard across my cheek.

"What the fuck—" The words come out of my mouth involuntarily.

There is something wrong with this child, I swear.

He stares at me with angry eyes and hits me again.

"That's enough, Billy!"

I grab his hand, and we walk home, Billy trying his best to catch up to my stride. I'm furious. My child should not be acting out like this and hitting me.

I clasp his hand since Billy is trying to free himself from my grip. "Hurt, Mom. Hurt," he whimpers.

"Well, if you didn't try to get away, I wouldn't be so rough."

I look around and see a car I hadn't seen earlier parked on the edge of our street. Since the glare is hitting the front window, I can't tell if anyone is sitting at the wheel. It's unusual for cars to be parked on our small street, so it looks out of place. Most houses are tucked in, and each one has more than plenty of space for parking.

If anyone was sitting inside the car, they must have seen the entire scene with Billy unfold.

Shit.

I grab Billy in my arms and hasten my steps toward the house. Only when we enter do I sigh in relief. I put Billy down, and he runs to his toy room.

At least he has a room to escape to. I feel entirely depleted. I need a blunt or a glass of wine, or anything to calm down.

I plop down on the couch and rest my arm on my forehead while I reflect on my shitty life. It's been anything but easy. I mean, I love Billy. He's my life but being a single mom sucks ass. He wasn't planned, and for me, that has made it feel even harder.

Because, when you plan a child, you really want it,

from the depth of your heart. You prepare for them physically and mentally and you hop on the pregnancy bandwagon and hope your baby will come out alive and healthy. And you cherish every moment being pregnant—you download the app to follow the baby's growth from a tiny little peppercorn to a watermelon.

Not me. I didn't find out Billy was inside me until he'd grown into an orange. It shook me to my core. It was too late to have an abortion, and giving him up for adoption didn't cross my mind. I thought I'd just wing it. I had this stupid idea that everything would be easy when the baby was born.

What the fuck was I smoking? Single motherhood is hard. Like, *really* hard.

I remove my arm from my forehead and open my eyes. Billy's voice carries across the house. As usual, he's doing his best to talk to his toys.

It occurs to me I need to get him a birthday gift. A belated one, of course. But I need to see what the balance in my checking account looks like.

I stand up from the couch and approach my old computer on the kitchen table. When I open it, unease rushes over me, as if invisible hands are about to strangle me.

Something is amiss.

I just can't point my finger on what it is. It's just the feeling in my gut telling me so.

In the browser, I type in my bank's website and enter my username and password. In the back of my mind, I should have at least $4,000—partial proceeds from my rental place. The money gets automatically deposited each first of the month, and today is September 3rd. So, money should technically be there.

That feeling in the pit of my stomach is right: I'm nearly broke, and the rental money has not arrived in my checking account.

I throw my hands in the air and whisper, "Fuck."

I need to call Gabriel.

CHAPTER 23

Claire

NONE OF THIS MAKES SENSE.

Gabriel has always been diligent in making rent payment on time. What happened this month? I can't think of one reason, since, for the past three years, the rent payment was always on time. Never skipped a beat.

I locate my phone and type in my password with my shaky hands. I scroll down to Gabriel's phone number and push Call. It rings once and goes straight to voicemail.

"Darn it."

I dial again, only to get the same results—straight to voicemail.

Do I have Charlotte's phone number? I don't, of course. Gabriel would have never allowed me to get close to his wife or there would be dire consequences.

"Fuck!" I yell and throw my phone into the wall. Luckily, my phone has a protective case, so it doesn't shatter into a million pieces. But it helps a little with my rising anger.

I run to Billy's toy room and scoop him up.

"What doing, Mommy?"

Billy sounds scared and doesn't know why I'm handling him so roughly. I don't mean to, but anger has a tight grip on me.

"Sorry, buddy. I'm going to take you for a ride."

Billy is fighting me hard and trying to get out of my hands, but I'm a lot stronger. In my cloudy haze, I'm not paying much attention to what I'm doing. I am on autopilot. I put him in his car seat and buckle him up, then run to the other side of the car. Billy isn't happy with me, but he'll calm down once the car gets moving. The engine goes on, and I sigh in relief. I really don't want a repeat of the car tank being empty again.

I head toward the main street and see the same car in the same spot as earlier. Since I'm driving fast, I only notice a silhouette of a figure sitting at the wheel, but I can't tell if it's a man or a woman or what they look like. As I drove by, I'd felt their eyes upon me.

Billy's crying from the back snaps me out of my thoughts. I try to calm him down while concentrating on the road. The echo of his voice in the car is overwhelming. I cringe.

"Billy," I scream to overpower his voice. "Stop crying! I'll get you some ice cream later."

I'll say anything to make him quiet.

"No ice cweam." he yells back.

Calming Billy down is futile, as always. Sometimes I wish I could leave him with a neighbor or a friend for just half an hour, but it's not an option for me. Plus, this is so last minute, I doubt anyone would be generous enough to take him.

"Hey, listen." I do my best to use my calm voice. "We're going to a place with a swimming pool. Maybe we can do a little swimming. What do you say?"

Billy can't swim, and neither can I, but there's something alluring and fun about swimming pools. I'm hoping the idea of hanging by the pool would distract him.

Billy seems to be tired of his own crying. He's sitting in his car seat, looking depleted. His lips frown and his eyes stare at nothing.

He says nothing.

"Listen, we're going two towns over. I just need to check something, and we'll go back home. And then you can play with your toys again, okay?"

I see him give me a look in the rearview mirror before he settles his gaze on the window.

He remains quiet.

I don't need to tell him I'm on the mission to go to the house and look for Gabriel. I know he won't be happy to see me there, but what other choice do I have? They owe me money for September's rent, and it's strange he missed it—and that he's not answering his calls.

Half an hour later, we arrive. I turn around and see Billy, sound asleep. I wish I hadn't cut his hair and ruined his cute, angel-like looks, but that's what he gets for being so resistant. Oh, well.

I leave him sleeping in his seat and exit the car. The sunset is hiding behind the horizon already, and the purple and orange sky looks breathtaking. But I'm not here to enjoy the sunset. I'm here to chase down the family I've rented this big house to.

I look through the gate and notice something is amiss. All the lights in the house are off, and everything looks so ghostly. In fact, it appears as if the house is no longer inhabited, because there isn't one sign of life that tells me otherwise. Where are all the kids' toys in the front yard? The trampoline. The slide. Charlotte was good at playing with the kids in the front yard. I'm pretty sure there was a swing at the front.

I take the key out of my pocket and put it in the gate's main door. The key doesn't fit. I take a better look and confirm this is the key I've always used. Did Gabriel change the lock? My stomach churns. Why would he do it? Does he think this is funny?

I rattle the key a little harder, but nothing happens.

The gate is too high for me to jump over to check the premises. I couldn't leave Billy in the car alone, anyway.

I look up and close my eyes. When I open them, the sky looks more pronounced. Angrier. At the periphery of my vision, an object pulls me in, and I turn to my left to see what it is.

A sign that says FOR SALE.

I gasp in disbelief.

An enormous cry coming from the inside car gets my attention.

Billy.

I survey the house one last time and head over to the car. Billy's voice gets louder as I get closer. I open the door. "Billy, what is it?"

He's covered in vomit, and his eyes are puffy from crying.

"Oh, Jesus," I whisper. "Let's get you home, buddy."

I take the wipes from the back seat and clean him as best as I can. I rush to my seat, put the car into gear, and head home. As I drive, Billy's whining becomes the distant soundtrack to my panicked realizations.

The house sale can only mean two things: The family has moved out because Charlotte has found out about the unthinkable—that Gabriel has cheated on her with me.

The odds of this are high, I imagine. But Gabriel is clever. He has pulled worse stunts in the past before.

Or two, and this is more likely: Lynn has found out from prison that I've rented her house and has hired someone to take care of it.

In my gut, I can't say which one feels worse.

CHAPTER 24

Susan

IT'S past ten in the morning, and Billy is a no show.

I wonder what's keeping him away from school today. The parents are not obligated to inform us their kids are not coming to school, and frankly, I don't expect Claire to do it even if she had to. But it would be nice if she did, so I don't have to think and worry about it all day.

There's been only one time he didn't show up at school on time. It was when Claire took him to the beach on a whim, but didn't tell us about it until after the fact.

The cutoff arrival time is 9:30.

I take my phone from the desk drawer and open my screen. Before I send a text, I glance around to ensure no one is looking. It's not a strict policy, but it's an unspoken rule that we shouldn't use our personal cell phones during the day, only for emergencies, so I don't want to be disrespectful. I send a quick text:

No show today.

I put my phone back in the drawer and sit back. Maybe I should call Claire and ask if Billy is okay, but I don't want her to be suspicious.

It's quiet, so I open the search browser on my computer and enter her name in the search box.

I find one entry under her name, but that's not her. I see absolutely nothing under her name, as if she doesn't even exist. Isn't she a real estate agent? Wouldn't there be some kind of online presence when she lists houses?

My brother tells me not to bother looking up more information about her, but I'm dying of curiosity.

I can't shake the feeling that something is off. My fingers hover over the keyboard, itching to dig deeper. But I know that crossing this line could lead to trouble. After all, I'm a teacher, not a detective.

I force myself to close the browser tab, but my mind races with possibilities. Why is there no trace of her? And why didn't she inform the school today?

Someone calling my name down the hallway startles me. I jump in my seat, quickly shutting the laptop. It's just a student with a question, but my heart is pounding as if I've been caught red-handed. The kid just wants to know if tomorrow is a pajama day. Sure, why not, I tell him.

I try to focus on the rest of the day, but the mystery of

Billy's absence gnaws at me. What if something happened to him? What if Claire is hiding something? The possibilities are endless, and they all lead me down a dark path.

By the time school ends, I'm no closer to answers, but my resolve has only strengthened. As I walk out of the building, I decide to take a different route home. One that just so happens to pass by Billy's house. I've jotted down his address from the school records.

I tell myself it's just to ease my mind. But deep down, I know it's more than that. Something is wrong, and I need to know what.

CHAPTER 25

Claire

BILLY ISN'T FEELING well today. He has some kind of bug that has glued him to his bed. He's been throwing up since yesterday and he doesn't have any appetite. I called his doctor this morning, but they tell me he must have a virus, and there's nothing they can do for him. They further advised me to give him lots of liquid and have him rest until the virus is gone. Warm chicken soup would be best.

But I don't have chicken soup at home. Or any kind of soup, for that matter.

Billy is in bed, sleeping soundly, and I go in often to check on him. My day has gone to waste, since I can't meet with clients or show them any houses. Since I don't make enough on commissions, I don't have a personal assistant to step in and help me. And my colleagues? Well, there's only a handful, and none of them have been friendly or kind. I cut my losses and do my best to conduct whatever business I can drum up online and via phone.

It's almost noon, and Billy is still asleep. I approach our bed and give him a quick kiss on the cheek. He doesn't even flinch. He must be in a deep sleep.

As I walk through the door, my phone rings. I've been waiting for an anxious client to get back to me on a rental, so I expect that's a call from her.

It's not.

I stop in my tracks when I see the call is from Gabriel. I run to the kitchen, so I can take the call away from the bedroom so as not to wake Billy. Before I answer, I plop down on the rickety chair.

"Where the hell are you?" I say with a loud whisper through my clenched teeth.

"Why, hello to you, too." Gabriel sounds amused.

"I don't have time for niceties. You owe me an explanation. What is going on, Gabriel?"

"Hold on."

I hear movements in the background and a door closing, then a stream of cars whooshing by in the background. Then Gabriel's voice reemerges. "Hey."

"Where the hell are you? Tell me what's going on."

"I'm in Texas. We just moved here."

He sounds so calm, as if he's telling me what he just ate for lunch.

Me? I can hardly breathe when I hear the news, and I hold on to the table so not to fall.

"Are you there?"

"Yes..." I can barely get the words out of my mouth. "What are you doing in Texas? Why didn't you tell me?"

"Listen, I think Charlotte was getting suspicious about us again. I just couldn't take that risk. And I swear her father is after me again. I think someone has been following me for the past few months."

"But I haven't seen you in ages!" I try not to scream. "I don't know what you're talking about, Gabriel. It's not like you're cheating on Charlotte again."

Pause. Well, unless he's cheating on her with someone else.

"Why didn't you tell me you were moving out? My life depends on the rent money." I swear I'm about to cry.

He doesn't even miss a beat. "I don't need to tell you anything. I'm calling to tell you that you probably won't be hearing from me ever again."

Another stab to my guts. "What? Why are you saying that?" I can hardly compose myself. I take a deep breath and continue. "What about Billy?" I plead with him again.

"Stop it already! We've talked about this a million times." Gabriel's voice is etched with anger. "Billy is not my child."

Here we go again.

Gabriel and I have been in a relationship on and off, and while not official, we saw each other often enough and had sex. Our relationship worked well, since I'm not one to get tied to someone. And it worked for Gabriel, because ... well, because he needed to feed his power and ego, and I was just his pawn.

But Billy *is* his child, because I was not involved with anybody else around the time I got pregnant. Gabriel keeps denying it because he's scared.

"We're not going over this again, are we, Gabriel? How dare you deny your own child?" I'm so angry, I could punch something just about now.

"And like we said before, there's zero evidence I am the father. And you won't convince me otherwise."

Gabriel is chickenshit and scared of his father-in-law. Imagine if he found out about his extramarital child? No amount of money would help redeem him.

Gabriel has refused to undergo DNA testing. Even if he was the father, he's told me frequently it would have been a mistake.

We keep silent for a while, and all I hear is the continuous rush of cars. Frustrated, angry tears well up in my eyes.

"What about the house? Did you put it up for sale?"

Like everything else, Gabriel is pretty crafty and has an army of people doing things for him that are more than shady. He's rich, so I guess he can do whatever he wants.

Like, change my names multiple times. He's changed my names to protect my identity while he's being deceitful to his wife. But the more I think about it, the more I realize that it's just to protect himself.

He scoffs. "What? No. That was not me. And by the

way, thanks for renting us the house. It's nice, but there's something creepy about it. I can't put my finger on it."

He says that after three years of living there?

"Don't change the subject now. The house is fine. If you didn't put it up for sale, then who did?"

"How should I know? But I need to tell you..." Someone opens the door and calls his name. They have a brief conversation, then Gabriel gets on the phone again. "Hey, listen, I have to go now. Like I said, this is the last time we speak. Good luck with everything."

With that, the phone line goes dead.

CHAPTER 26

Claire

GABRIEL IS FOREVER GONE from my life.

I place my head in my hands and cry.

Feeling woozy, I head to the living room and lie down on the couch. Billy is still sound asleep, and I'm grateful. Tears stream down my face as I tightly shut my eyes. I reflect on the first time Gabriel and I met.

I'd been strolling down the beach when a handsome man met my gaze and said hello. He'd asked me if I was from around here and if I could recommend any good restaurants. Later, I learned it was just a ploy to get our conversation started, which worked.

During our introductions, Gabriel told me he was single, even though he was married with two small children. After that evening, we met a few more times, purely for fun. From a man like Gabriel, most women would demand a relationship, a sacrifice that meant leaving his wife and family. But with me, he was safe because I didn't want any of it. I'm not the type to get tied down.

That arrangement worked perfectly—until it didn't.

After a month, the truth came out, and I learned for the first time that Gabriel was married. He confessed that his wife and her father were suspicious. His father-in-law, a former army general, kept a tight leash on Gabriel, watching his every move to ensure he didn't hurt his daughter or their kids. But Gabriel had so much money, he could get away with more than the general could ever imagine.

It's almost as if he wanted to see how far he could go without being discovered.

Around the same time, my financial situation was precarious. I didn't want to ask my stepfather for help, but I was on the brink of homelessness. So instead, I'd told Gabriel I needed him, and we quickly reached a deal.

I convinced him to rent Lynn's mansion, which had all the amenities he and his family were looking for. I was living there alone, after all.

It felt empty after my mother was carted off to prison.

While I could have rented out some rooms, I don't enjoy sharing my space with strangers. My real estate deals weren't bringing in much income, and I needed to find another way to make money. So, I moved out, found a smaller place, and rented Lynn's mansion to Gabriel.

He agreed on one condition: I had to change my name

to conceal my identity, as his father-in-law had found out who I was. To comply with his wishes, I changed my name to Claire. Gabriel, like a Godfather figure, wielded significant influence and had connections in every corner of the world. It didn't take long for me to make the change.

Changing my name helped prevent the wife or the father-in-law from discovering the affair. It could make it more difficult for anyone who might be suspicious to trace our interactions. But even more so, Gabriel was manipulative and controlling, and he wanted to have me under his thumb.

I needed him to keep living in the house and making rent payments on time. Because renting it out was not an easy ordeal. No one wanted to live in it until I met Gabriel. Those hefty monthly payments came in handy when Billy was enrolled in daycare. And now, because Gabriel has moved to another state, I'll have to deal with the son I never wanted and the new name, along with the soon-to-be accumulated debt.

I've gone too far with Gabriel. I never should have let him control me. I just thought it seemed harmless at the time.

Because the truth of the matter is, this is not who I am. I long to be motherless, and my real name is not Claire.

My name is Lucy, damnit.

I should take pride in my true identity. But Gabriel had me under his thumb, because he knew he could. He knew I needed him.

A bolt of unease leads me to prop myself up and sit

down. I light a joint to relax. It's an excellent opportunity to sit around and do nothing while Billy is sleeping. I do my best to avoid smoking in front of him, but today is the exception to the rule. Today, I need to escape from my nightmares.

After a few puffs, I'm lulled to sleep and enter the dreamland.

I'm standing in the middle of an endless field, the grass waving gently under a pale, sickly moon. The sky is a bruised, angry purple, with clouds churning and shifting like restless spirits. In the distance, I see a small, dilapidated house, its windows dark and vacant. My legs feel heavy, like they're submerged in molasses, but I force myself to move forward.

As I get closer, I notice a person standing in front of the house. It's my father. His back is to me, but I recognize the broad shoulders; the way he holds himself. I try to call out, but the oppressive silence swallows my voice. Panic grips my chest. I need to reach him, to touch him, to make sure he's real.

My feet finally find solid ground, and I break into a run. The distance between us seems to stretch, the house receding no matter how fast I move. I scream, but the sound is torn from my throat, leaving only a hoarse whisper.

Then, suddenly, I'm there. I'm right behind him. I reach out, my fingers trembling, and touch his shoulder. He turns slowly, his face shrouded in shadow.

"Dad?" My voice is small, childlike. He looks down at

me, and I see his eyes are hollow voids that swallow the light.

"Why did you abandon me?" I ask.

He doesn't answer. Instead, he turns and walks away. I try to follow, but my feet are rooted to the ground. I watch helplessly as he gets farther and farther away, his figure growing smaller until it's just a speck on the horizon.

The sky darkens, the moon vanishing behind thick clouds. I'm alone in the field, the grass now a twisted, writhing mass of serpents. They coil around my legs, pulling me down into the earth. I struggle, but the more I fight, the tighter they squeeze.

"Dad!" I scream, but it's too late. He's gone. The ground swallows me whole, and I'm plunged into darkness.

A slight movement wakes me up. Something is tugging at my arm sleeve. I hear a small voice, "Mommy, Mommy."

It's Billy. He's awake. I peel my heavy eyes open and gaze at Billy standing next to me. He's still looking ill.

"Hey, Billy, what is it?" I sit up and rub my eyes.

"Billy hungyee."

He's on the verge of crying. He must be hungry, as he hasn't eaten since last night. I can't remember what's in the fridge, but there could be some leftovers. He's clinging to me, and I try my best to get out of his grip. I stand up and go to the kitchen with Billy trudging behind me. A carton of milk sits on the shelf, but I'm not sure if it's still good. I grab it and point it toward Billy.

"Kiddo, do you want milk?" My voice is coarse from sleeping.

Billy bursts into tears. "I don't want milk."

I put the milk back on the shelf and slam the fridge door shut. Damn it. When was the last time I went grocery shopping, anyway? I don't even remember. I open the kitchen cabinet and see a jar of peanut butter. I shake my head in dismissal. Billy is a pain in the ass with food. He hates peanut butter.

I try it anyway. "What do you want to eat, then? Peanut butter and jelly sandwich?"

Billy screams and gets down on the floor, banging his head against it.

At first, I stay rooted to my spot, unable to move as I watch his body convulse in front of my eyes. This isn't normal, is it? I've been told toddler years can be tricky, and that kids pull off tantrums on a whim, but Billy is about to hurt himself terribly.

I grab him from behind and lift him up in the air. Now I'm wide awake, and I try to take control of the situation.

"Billy, tell me what you wanna eat. Tell me!" I raise my voice and shake him in my arms, growing impatient with him.

But Billy just can't stop screaming. And it's too much for my ears. I carry him to the bedroom and place him on the bed. "Stop screaming! I'm going to prepare you a sandwich and you better eat it. Do you hear me?"

I storm out of the room and head to the kitchen and find things to prepare him a sandwich. Billy's cry carries through the house. He keeps wailing. And there's nothing I can do to stop him.

CHAPTER 27

Susan

SECOND DAY IN A ROW, Billy is a no show.

I walk to his classroom to check he hasn't arrived late, but I don't see Billy. I signal for Rebeca to come over, and she stands up and approaches me.

"Everything okay?" She frowns when she sees my panicked face.

"Yeah, yeah. Everything's fine. Just wanted to double check Billy isn't here. Is he?" I look over her shoulder for good measure.

She shakes her head. "No. He's definitely not here." She squints. "Why, is he okay?"

I pause and consider her question. I don't want her to worry, but I feel I should say something.

"That's the thing, I don't know. He hasn't shown up two days in a row, and I'm worried."

When I drove by their house yesterday, I saw nothing unusual. The lights were on, but I didn't notice any movements inside. I sat in my car for ten minutes, but I didn't want to worry Scott I would be too late for dinner.

Rebecca places her hand on my shoulder. "Listen, you worry too much. I'm sure he's okay." She smiles, only to placate me. I think she's happy Billy didn't make it, because he's almost impossible to manage.

But now I have other reasons to worry.

I'm growing more and more nervous, and I don't know what to think of it all. I can tell right away when something is amiss. But I do my best to mask my worry in front of Rebecca and offer a smile back. "You know, you're absolutely right. There's probably nothing to worry about."

A child cries, and Rebecca is instantly on alert. "I gotta go."

I watch her kneel and talk to the crying child whose toy was just confiscated by another. I go back to my desk and find our Assistant Director, Shelly, sitting there, poring over some records. She's in her own world and doesn't quite notice me until I approach the desk. She looks as if she's about to stand up and offer me her seat, but I stop her with my hand. "No need." I open the drawer and pull out my phone. "I need to make an emergency phone call."

"Everything okay?" Shelly asks.

"Yep."

The bathroom is around the corner, and I walk in,

eager to call my brother. I dial, and he picks up on a second ring tone.

"Heya," he says. His voice exudes joy and positivity.

"I'm hiding in the bathroom at work." I'm whispering, though I know no one can hear me. "I'm calling to see if you've got anything?"

"Working on it!" he says.

I'm so lucky I can rely on him. My big brother has been my biggest supporter ever since we were children. He's a few years older than me, but he has always been so protective. And so loving.

"Okay, excellent. When should I expect to get something?"

"I think I have enough material, but I need to put it all together. So, say, tomorrow?"

An involuntary smile crosses my face. "Tomorrow would be great."

We hang up, and I exit the bathroom with a giant sense of relief. Tomorrow will be different.

Tomorrow is the day when some lives will change.

CHAPTER 28

Claire

BY THE EVENING, Billy has calmed down.

We're sitting in the living room with the TV on. I put on *Paw Patrol*, Billy's favorite, to keep him distracted. He's sitting on the couch, legs akimbo, his shoulders slightly slouched, and his face resting on his hands. His eyes are watery from the fever he's been fighting. Earlier, he had a bite of a sandwich I made him and a couple of strawberries. I always pray he'll eat more, but he doesn't. Sometimes I wonder if all those tantrums result from his poor diet.

His eyes are intent on the TV, and he blinks every once in a while, releasing freshly new tears. Sometimes I feel sorry for Billy. He doesn't have grandparents who would give him the love and attention most children deserve.

Fred, my adopted stepfather, is no longer in the

picture. I never imagined there would come a day when Fred wouldn't be the central figure in my life. He raised me with so much love and dedication after Mary passed away, doing his best to fill the void her death left behind.

But as time went on, things changed. I remember the first time I told him I wanted to meet Jimmy, my biological father. The look of apprehension in his eyes was something I couldn't shake. It was as if he feared losing his place in my heart, but he never said anything to discourage me. He just smiled that sad, knowing smile and said, "Whatever you need to do to find yourself, Lucy."

The more I pursued my own path, the more I sensed the distance growing between us. Organizing the housewarming party without him felt like a betrayal, but I was too caught up in my excitement to see it then.

In our last phone conversation, Fred had the nerve to tell me I'd changed. I wasn't the same person he raised and loved. But people don't look at themselves often enough. He didn't realize how smitten he was by his second wife, who holds him by the balls. Sometimes I wonder how he could move on so fast if he'd truly ever loved Mary.

But I don't want to dwell on it. I'm trying my best to focus on what's in front of me.

And Lynn? Don't even get me started on her.

What a disappointment she is. After I learned she'd murdered Jimmy, all I could think of was the times she'd led me to believe he was still alive: giving me his phone number and email address in order to get in touch with him. Telling me they were getting divorced. She treated me like I was an idiot.

There's something about her persistent lying that didn't sit well with me. She could have come clean, and she and I could have figured something out. But no, she made a fool out of me instead. It makes my blood boil when I think about it.

It's no surprise I've chosen not to visit her in jail. Because of that choice, Lynn has removed me from her will and the house deed, no longer giving me access to any of her money. It just shows you how much she really loved me. But her actions put me in a bind, so I had no choice but to be creative. I had to come up with the plan to make more money, and renting her mansion was it.

But I don't have that option, either, now. I'm totally screwed.

Billy fidgets on the couch, and his eyes begin to droop.

"Billy, do you want to go to bed?"

"No!"

Most of the time, Billy refuses to go to bed, even though he can barely hold his head up. His pale face is radiant from the TV reflection. I gaze at the wall clock and see it's nine. Billy should go to bed. And because he still looks sick, I'm reluctant to send him to school tomorrow. Besides, my job has been eerily slow. And it scares the crap out of me.

I approach Billy and scoop him up. "Let's go to bed, love."

He's resistant at first, but he gives in under my strength. I carry him to the bed and put him down.

"Do you want milk before you fall asleep?"

Billy squints at me, barely awake. "No."

I caress his hair and give him a kiss on the cheek. It's been a hard couple of days for Billy, but I trust he will bounce back soon.

"Sleep well, and you will feel better tomorrow. Pinky promise."

I don't think he knows what "pinky promise" means, but this is the phrase Mary often used when I was a child. Whenever she promised something, she followed through. That's what I loved about her.

I miss her so much.

Billy turns around to his side to face the wall and says nothing. He's ready to enter dreamland.

The glare from the streetlight outside the window is overbearing. I approach the window to close the curtains, and I stop in my tracks when I see someone standing nearby. I can't tell if it's a man or a woman, or whether they're looking in my direction. But I get this strange feeling that they're here for a reason.

The shadow shifts, and the contours of the body become better defined. It's definitely a man. He waves at me, then proceeds toward the street. I squint to see if I recognize him, but judging by his movements, I'm sure I've never seen him before.

Then a scary thought occurs to me.

He might have been watching me this whole time.

CHAPTER 29

Susan

I TIPTOE through the door of the school as if I'm on eggshells and look around to check if anyone is here. It's only five thirty in the morning. I've left Scott in bed, sleeping, and a note next to him to let him know I had to go to work earlier than usual. He typically wakes up at the same time as me, and we have coffee together and chat, or plan for dinner. He always wants to know if I have special requests. I typically don't.

Today, I'm not even thinking about eating. My stomach is tied into knots.

Because today is a special day—if everything works as it should.

I really have no reason to be here so early, other than

my nerves not letting me sleep this morning. I walk around mindlessly. Our first child usually arrives around six in the morning. While I wait for the first arrivals, I busy myself in the kitchen, moving the merchandise from one shelf to another. It's not my typical job, but I'll do anything to distract my mind.

A voice behind me startles me. "Hey, you're here already?"

It's Shelly. I put my hand on my chest, feeling my heart pumping like a drum. "Oh my God, you scared me."

"Sorry. You're early." She looks around. "Is there something going on today?"

"Oh, no. No." I shake my head. "I just couldn't sleep last night, so I thought I'd head to work early."

"I hear you." She heads for the coffee machine to brew a fresh carafe. "I didn't sleep that well, either. I think it's this weather."

It has been heavy and humid the past few nights. But it's not the reason I couldn't sleep.

After we've exchanged a few words, we go back to our respective corners. Families drop off their children, several of them crying and reluctant to leave their mom or dad behind. I've seen it all.

But I'm not paying much attention this morning. I'm absentminded and focused on one thing only.

The wait is killing me. I buzz around the space, going from one classroom to another, and I watch the kids play. Billy's absence is noticed, as there's no rising tension and fear in the classroom. At least that's one positive.

At lunchtime, I walk to the coffee shop around the corner and order myself a simple sandwich. I'm barely eating at the moment, but I have to, because what's ahead of me requires strength. Mental and physical.

On my way back to the school, I breathe in the fresh air of the distant ocean. The summer is at its tail end, but I'm looking forward to witnessing the foliage. New England looks like a living painting in the fall.

The breathing centers me, and I feel better. I muster all my mental strength and tell myself I can do the task ahead of me.

As I walk back, my phone chimes, and I pause for a minute to see what it is. A text message. Is it him? My thoughts run to the worst-case scenario: he wants to let me know things aren't going as planned and we need to abort all the activities. Re-evaluate.

With a shaky hand, I pull out my phone from my purse and sigh when I see the text is from Scott.

> Hey, you left early this morning.
> Everything okay?

He makes me smile. He's always so concerned and thoughtful. I respond and tell him everything is okay, even though it's far from the truth. But I don't want him to worry unnecessarily.

When I arrive back at daycare, it's eerily quiet. It's nap time and the kids are asleep. I sit at my desk and wait. I kill my time by checking out the news and browsing the internet. These quiet times are a welcome reprieve to a busy day. Around two o'clock, the expected visitor walks through the door. My heart beats a little faster, and my palms sweat.

Our mailman, Barnie.

Barnie has been our mailman for nearly a decade. A man in his late fifties, always with a cheerful disposition. When he comes in, it's as if a family member is visiting. He looks tired, but he skillfully masks the tiredness by always being so cheerful.

"Hey there," he says.

"Hi, Barnie." My voice cracks, and I clear my throat to steady my nerves.

He approaches my desk and sifts through the mail in his hands. "Well, today doesn't look like a lot, but you've got a few pieces here."

I crane my neck to check the pile. I don't want to appear too eager or nervous about it.

"Wonderful," I say.

He places the mail on my desk and looks at me. "How are you doing today? Are the kids behaving?"

I let out a chuckle. "Oh, always. You know how it is around here." I say that, but I know he doesn't.

"My granddaughter is starting kindergarten this year. I can't believe it. They grow up so fast."

I nod and say nothing. I'm usually fine with check-ins and meaningless banter, but not today. I need to get to the mail ASAP. Barnie is staring at me, and when he doesn't get a response, he tells me he's on his way. "Well, see you tomorrow at the same time. Stay cool."

"I will. Thanks, Barnie. See you tomorrow."

As soon as he crosses the door's threshold, I leap onto the desk and grab the mail pile. My heart is about to burst from beating too fast. I turn around and run to my corner office.

CHAPTER 30

Susan

I RARELY COME to my office. I spend most of my time at the front desk, greeting the families, fielding their burning questions, addressing their concerns. That's the biggest part of my job. Sometimes I forget I have an office. But today, it comes in extremely handy.

Before I close the door, I peek through to see if anyone is watching me, and thankfully, nobody is. I close the door and lock it.

With the pile of mail in my hand, I sit at my desk and sift through my haul until I come across a small yellow envelope. My name is written across it with a Sharpie, in that familiar handwriting. No return address. The sender is mysterious.

But not to me.

I grab an envelope opener from a cup next to my computer. Seconds later, a thumb drive is sitting on the palm of my hand.

I feel its smooth edges in my hand, but inside, I'm a wreck, and my emotions are a whirlwind. My computer is on, so I touch the mouse to bring the screen to life. I enter the password and, seconds later, I look at my screen with a zillion folders spread around the desktop.

The thumb drive fits perfectly into the USB slot, and another folder appears on the desktop. I close my eyes to compose myself before the storm.

Breathe in. Breathe out.

Okay, I'm ready. I think.

With a steady hand, I open the folder and see one file contained inside. A movie. My heart beats faster, but I have no choice. I must do it.

With one click, the file opens. My fingers tremble as I press the play button, knowing what's coming, but unable to look away. The video starts with a mundane scene: a living room, slightly messy, toys scattered on the floor. But the air feels heavy, like something sinister lurks just beneath the surface.

The camera shifts, and there they are—mother and child. The child, a toddler, sits on the couch, eyes wide and wary. I can see the fear etched on his face, a stark contrast to the mother's cold, hard expression. My stomach knots. She stands before the child, poking him on his shoulders. He tries to dodge her touch, but she is persistent. Her moves are harsh, and the tone is unmistakable, dripping with venom.

I watch, breath caught in my throat, as she raises her hand. I want to scream, to reach through the screen and stop her. But I'm frozen, powerless. The child flinches, curling into himself, as if trying to disappear. My hands grip the edge of the table, knuckles white. My skin feels hot, a flush of anger mixed with a sickening sense of helplessness.

The scene shifts again. The mother grabs the child's arm, yanking him roughly off the couch. My heart races, and I feel a surge of nausea. The child stumbles, trying to keep up, but the grip is too tight. I can almost feel it, the sting of it, as if it's happening to me. My eyes sting with tears.

Poor Billy.

The video mercifully cuts off, leaving me in silence. The image has burned itself into my mind. I sit there, panting, my whole body trembling. The room feels colder now, the darkness pressing in. I close my eyes, trying to shake off the lingering horror, but it clings to me, wrapping around my chest like a vise.

I open my eyes and stare at the dark screen, my reflection ghostly. I feel sick, an overwhelming urge to do something, anything. But all I can do is sit here, trapped in this moment, the image of that terrified child singed into my memory.

I take a deep breath, but it does little to calm the storm

inside me. I reach for the laptop, hesitating before closing it.

I've never done anything like what I'm about to do, but there's a first for everything. I look up the number online, grab my phone, and dial.

It's time to save Billy.

CHAPTER 31

Claire

DUSK HAS SETTLED IN, and calm has enveloped the neighborhood. Someone rings the doorbell. I immediately wonder if it's the person who was watching me from outside earlier. Maybe they're lost. Maybe they need something. The doorbell rings again.

Billy is sitting on the floor watching TV. With the second ring of the bell, he protests against the noise and hits the floor hard with his little hands. I want to calm him down, but the doorbell rings again. It's better to open the door and put a stop to Billy's aggravation.

I look through the peephole and see two people standing on the other side. A man and a woman. They're both dressed up and they have stern looks on their faces.

I've never seen them before, and I can't even guess who they are.

Well, just this past month, I forgot to pay my electricity bill, so maybe they're here to settle it in person. Unusual, but not impossible. Before they ring the bell again, I open the door. They look at me as if they're surprised to see me. The man raises his eyebrows and scrunches his face. He doesn't look happy.

The woman has a poker face and seems to be the one in charge.

"Are you Claire Robinson?"

That's a loaded question. Because I'm not sure what the answer is anymore.

"Yes?" It sounds more like a question than an affirmation. Billy isn't helping the matter. He's in the living room, crying, and I can barely concentrate on what I'm saying. Or thinking.

"My name is Amanda Blake, and this is Eric Collins. We're from Child Protective Services. May we come in?"

My heart beats a little faster, but I'm in a daze. I'm not sure I am processing or hearing her correctly. Child Protective Services? It's got to be a mistake.

"What do you want?" I ask.

"May we come in?"

I turn around and see Billy sitting on the floor in a calmer state. He's looking at me with a fearful expression on his face, probably wondering what the two strangers are doing here.

After some hesitation, I open the door wide and tell them to come in.

They step in slowly, as if worried about walking on landmines. Their eyes dart all over my house as if they're looking for something. I don't like it. Their presence sends shivers through my body, and I fight a strong urge to run away.

The woman looks down at Billy, while he stares at her intently. "Hey, buddy." She kneels. "How are you?"

Billy makes an angry face and turns around, saying nothing. He's not interested in interacting with her. Though, that's Billy for you. His usual MO.

"Everything alright, Billy?" she presses on.

But Billy crosses his arms on his torso and does a 180, turning his back to her.

She stands up and instructs me to take Billy to his room, if possible. I feel my forehead creasing. "Why? Is there a problem?"

"We need to have a conversation privately without Billy in the room."

Instead of doing as she asked, I'm rooted to my spot, unable to move. I can feel a storm drawing closer, and I'm helpless to stop it or do anything about it.

"Claire?" She raises a brow and stares at me, as if she wants me to react.

"Fine." I shake my head as I approach Billy.

Billy is still pouting on the floor and does not want to be touched, even by me. He screams from the top of his lungs, and I do my best to silence him, "It's okay, buddy. How about we go to your room and play with your toys?"

But Billy won't budge.

I gaze at the two strangers, who are looking down at me, and observing. I feel like this is some kind of test I never signed up for. I grab Billy, and he resists my hard grip. He's like a venomous snake, swirling and twirling in my arms, trying to escape. But I'm a lot stronger than him.

I carry him to his playroom and tell him to stay. He's still crying and his voice is building a strange tension in my body. I feel like punching someone, and I surmise my rising anger has something to do with the strangers infiltrating my home.

Billy keeps crying and buries his face into the carpet. I can't watch or listen to him anymore, so I head out the door and close it behind me.

I storm back into the living room, where Amanda and Eric are whispering.

"How can I help you?" I say, doing my best to regulate my emotions.

"Can we sit down?" Amanda asks.

"Sure."

They sit down on the couch next to each other and lean forward. Nothing about their body language suggests they're here to relax and chit-chat. This is going to be a serious conversation.

"We're here to talk about Billy." Eric finally finds his voice. It sounds deep and authoritative. "We have received some tapes from someone anonymous, suggesting that you've neglected your son."

My jaw drops to the floor. My mouth is agape, and it's like someone has just jabbed a hammer right in my stomach. I'm breathless.

"This is obviously a big concern, and, as you know, it won't be tolerated. Children must be protected at all costs,"

Billy's screaming from the playroom, and I crane my neck in his direction, helpless. I don't know what to do anymore. The combination of shock coursing through my head and the old habit of doing little when Billy screams, is pinning me to the spot.

Amanda is playing with her hands, looking nervous. She moves her hair to the side and looks at Eric, as if she wants him to hurry.

"What video?" My voice is a whisper.

"A video that shows the way you have neglected Bill."

I follow Amanda's eyes that stop at the bag of weed under my table. Shit. That's the stash I got yesterday. Excellent stuff. Wasn't cheap. Are they going to take it away?

"We're not here to argue or ask many questions," Eric says, then pauses, as if making sure I'm paying attention. "We're here to take Billy away. He's not prospering or growing up in a healthy environment. Until you improve the living conditions and go through some parenting classes, Billy will remain in the state's custody."

Amanda has moved to the very edge of the seat and seems eager to collect Billy.

"What ... what are you saying?" Their words sound as if spoken in vacuum. I'm still doing my best to process what they're suggesting, but when Amanda stands up and walks toward the playroom, I barge toward her and scream, "No! No! You can't take my son! Don't take Billy away! Please!"

Amanda puts her hands up in defense, and suddenly I'm pulled away by Eric's powerful hands from behind.

Now I understand why there are two of them here.

Eric grabs my arms and locks them on my back, rendering me immobile. But I try to escape his grip, like a fish finding its way to the water. Eric is strong. "Stay calm," he tells me.

Seconds later, Amanda walks with Billy into the living room. Billy looks scared and confused, and he's staring at me with his enormous eyes.

"Mom." His voice cracks, but he looks strangely calm.

"Billy, Billy, don't leave me," I plead, but it lands on deaf ears.

As Billy walks through the living room with Amanda in tow, he fixes his gaze on me. They walk out the front door, hand in hand, while Eric holds me in his grip. He comes closer and places his lips near my ear. "It's the best for your child. Clean up your life and you can have him back. And don't do anything stupid once I release you. Got that?"

Tears stream down my face, and my nose runs. I can't wipe it with my tied hands.

Eric lets go of me and walks out the door, and I fall to the floor, sobbing uncontrollably. It's like someone's ripped apart a piece of me and all I want to do is die to avoid the pain.

I don't know how much time passes before I stand up. I drag myself to the window to see if the two strangers might have been just a mirage or a nightmare. There's nothing outside except for the usual trees and bushes standing nearby.

I walk from room to room, in a strange trance, looking for my son. I stop in my tracks to hear his voice, feel his beat, sense his presence. And I hear absolutely nothing.

That's when it hits me. Billy is gone.

Susan

DAYCARE CLOSES EARLY. All the parents have collected their children early in the anticipation of the long Labor Day weekend. I love it when we have an extra hour to spend at leisure on a beautiful day.

At least that's the way it should be.

I'm a wreck and can't concentrate. As I drive home, I nearly miss the red light and almost hit an incoming car from my left side. The loud honk gets me out of my stupor. I wave an apology to the driver.

The images of that video flash in front of my eyes, and I flinch. I've always suspected that Claire was negligent—she had to be—but there wasn't solid evidence until now.

I've done my part by calling CPS to report the abuse.

I suppose the grandmother could have made the call

into CPS, too, but she'd decided it was best that she be removed from the equation and conceal any suspicion. Plus, I could add my two cents and attest to Claire's late pickups and general lack of care for the child. Not to mention my growing concern for Billy, as he wasn't showing up to school day after day. It was easy to agree to do this favor.

I'm on standby to see what happens next. I just hope everything will work out as planned.

When I arrive home, Scott walks up to me in the hallway with a concerned look. "Hey, I've tried to call you multiple times, but you didn't pick up the phone. You really got me worried."

"Sorry about that," I say, without looking at him. I don't want him to see my distress. "It just got really busy during the day."

He approaches and gives me a hug. "Okay. Well, dinner will be ready shortly. Can I get you something to drink?"

My husband is funny. He acts like he's here to serve me, as if I can't open a wine bottle and pour it myself. But today, I let him.

Judging by the smell, it promises to be a delicious meal. Scott serves two bowls of meatballs and tomato sauce, and we sit at the dining table. I leave my phone out beside me, as I'm expecting a call.

As we eat in silence, my eyes dart between the phone and my food, and every once in a while, I gaze at Scott across from me, who's watching me with creased eyebrows.

He finally puts his fork down and slumps his shoulders. "What's the matter, honey? You seem distracted."

I was hoping he wouldn't ask. "I can't talk right now, but I promise I will. When the time is right."

He cocks his head. "Well, I trust you will tell me whatever is bothering you in due time."

I smile. "I will, honey. Don't worry."

Scott and I are solid. We've been married for almost three decades and never had children, so we've mainly just been worried about each other and ourselves. I suspect we will have a long life.

Just as I'm about to grab my fork and continue eating, my phone rings. Scott looks at me and offers a slight nod. I don't need his permission, but I still apologize for interrupting dinner when I get up to take the call.

I must take this call.

I run to my office on the corner of the first floor and close the door behind me. My brother's calling me.

Andrew.

My heart flutters in the anticipation of what news he is about to break. I hope for the best, but one never knows.

I pick up, sounding unsure of myself. "Hello?"

"All done. I'll see you for dinner next week." That's all he says before he hangs up the phone.

I exhale. I can finally relax.

CHAPTER 33

Claire

It's been only a couple of hours since they took Billy away from me.

I'm lying in bed, numb, unable to move. My arms are heavy and feel as if they belong to another entity. I'm thinking of going over to the living room and smoking a blunt, but I change my mind.

Now that Billy is gone, I reflect on all the mistakes I've made. The number of times I was late to pick him up at school, the mediocre meals I've made him, the lost opportunities for giving him kisses and hugs. The way I've been so impatient with him.

The amount of weed and alcohol I've consumed since he was born.

Now I realize I've been a terrible parent to him. Being

a single parent is difficult, sure, but it's no excuse not to make my child a priority.

A deep sense of regret and guilt washes over me. I squint my eyes in pain, and a stream of tears rolls down my cheeks. My chest feels heavy, and it heaves with sobs. I'm hyperventilating. Every attempt to catch a breath is a struggle. The sorrow is so heavy that I don't know how long it will take me to recover.

To get out of bed.

The images of my little boy are persistent in my mind: a little boy who grew up fatherless, troubled, for whatever reasons. I keep seeing those large droopy eyes that look at me as if asking for help. While I've done my best, I haven't done enough, and that is my biggest curse.

And as for those two people who took him away ... They took him so leisurely as if he were a piece of furniture. I rewind our conversation, focusing on the bit that sticks out to me.

They got a video from an anonymous sender.

Who could that be?

Is it the person who's been watching me lately? The person hiding behind the bushes in our backyard?

Gabriel could be pulling another prank. He is indeed a powerful force to be reckoned with. He probably never stopped believing that Billy was his son, but never wanted me to know that, either.

Has this been his plan all along? To move away to Texas with his family, then take Billy away?

If he did, I hate him, and I hope to haunt him down

someday. Ever since that phone call the other day, I've been trying to reach him and find another phone number to call him, but with no success. He's indeed clever.

The image of Billy leaving the house comes back to mind.

Before he left the house with the two strangers, he'd looked so confused, but not sad. It's as if he didn't know what to do or how to bid me farewell. As if he knew all along he was going to leave me and was okay with it.

That breaks my heart even more.

But there's one thing Billy does *not* know. I'm determined to clean up my life and find him. He is my son. I love him to pieces, and I will get him back.

Regardless of the price I need to pay.

PART THREE

CHAPTER 34

Three Months Later

MY PARTNER and I are sitting on the porch of my new home and sipping margaritas. I've only recently started drinking, but I never go overboard. One or two is enough. Today, we're celebrating the closing of my mansion by the ocean, and it's worth a drink or two.

It didn't take long to find a buyer, and the closing is always an endless task, but it's done now.

When my monthly lease expired at the rental place, I'd told Andrew I was ready to make a move and settle down with him. I will never forget the joy on his face when I told him. He gave me a big hug, picking me up from the ground and swirling me around.

A happy moment for both of us.

His house sits near the main golf course, a little way from the beach. It has three bedrooms and two-and-a-half bathrooms, with a stunning kitchen and a spacious living room next to it. A little den in the corner makes a perfect painting studio for me. I'll be dedicating my time to my new hobby. Aside from spending time with the loved ones, I've signed up to volunteer at a foundation concerning pregnant women dependent on drugs. I've already donated tens of thousands of dollars toward the cause. It's a real disease, but there is help available.

When I do nothing, I'll be resting my aging bones with my sweetie on the closed-in porch all year round while watching the earth's breathtaking beauty. There's a small pond next to the house, which gives a calming vibe when the sunset hits the purple sun rays. Our next-door neighbors are far enough away that we don't get to see often. I can see myself living here for the long haul.

Most importantly, there's enough room for our guests.

I pull my legs up over the railing, gripping the margarita glass in my hand. Andrew approaches me from behind me and puts his hands on my shoulders. He's so gentle, I can barely hear or feel him sometimes.

I crane my neck and turn around to look at him. "Hi, honey."

"Hi, sweetheart." He bends now and kisses the top of my head. If you really want to know what an actual sign of love looks like, it's when they kiss your greasy hair and don't find it repulsive.

"How's your margarita? Would you like another one?"

I look at my glass. It's nearly empty. "You know, why not?"

He gives me a little squeeze on a shoulder and takes my glass. "I'll be right back."

I smile. Andrew has been a dream. After solving his last case—mine—he has retired so he can golf and spend time with me and his family as much as he can. Because, when you age, you realize time slips away quickly. Knocking opportunities dwindle. Bones begin to shrink and hurt. There's no better way to transition into old age than enjoying time with loved ones and engaging in hobbies.

He comes back with a full glass and sits next to me.

"Is he still asleep?" I ask.

"I just checked on him. Yes, he's sound asleep."

Billy's naps have been longer than usual lately. He's having a growth spurt and has been a bottomless pit.

He'd moved in with us a couple of days after the Child Protective Services had removed him from his home. Since then, his weight had improved, and he looked a lot healthier. We've taken him to a psychologist who has helped him deal with his brittle emotions.

The psychologist has helped him parse out his feelings and learn good from bad. So far, Billy has made tremendous leaps, and his behavior has significantly improved. He now understands we are blood-related, and he calls me "grandma." I love hearing him say it. It melts my heart.

When CPS asked Lucy who Billy's father was, she told them it was Gabriel. It is no surprise he'd misled us when we met him and gave us the wrong name for his real estate agent.

Suzanne? There was no Suzanne! Gabriel wanted to divert us from the right path to ensure we took longer to locate Lucy until they'd all left for Texas.

At first, it was a shock to hear he was Billy's father, but then it made sense as far as their house rental arrangement —it appeared to be some kind of co-dependent deal: Lucy gets the money, and he gets the house, her, and all the control he needed to feed his ego. But he's still denied Billy as his child and doesn't want anything to do with him.

We did a DNA test after finding some fibers in the primary bathroom of the ocean mansion I'd recently sold. The DNA test confirmed it matched with Billy's.

Andrew's detective skills had paid off; he'd located Gabriel to inform him that Billy was indeed his son. We got something in writing to say that Gabriel would provide for Billy until he reaches eighteen. No parent should carry the burden of providing for their child alone.

According to our daily report, this news gave Lucy an immense relief, especially as she's struggled so much financially.

We also learned that Charlotte is divorcing Gabriel and getting full custody of their three children—thanks to some strings her father pulled.

As Billy's grandmother, I've looked out for him. I've

hugged and kissed him with every chance I'd got. I have all the time on earth to make things right for him, to make him happy.

To undo my own past mistakes.

Having him around makes me feel I'm getting another chance. All the mistakes I've made in life with my child are slowly being erased from my mind.

I'm filled with immense gratitude, and I pinch myself when happy tears fall down my face.

The people I should thank the most are Andrew and his sister, Susan. It's incredible that Susan mentioned an estate agent named Claire one day to Andrew, and before you know it, all the dots had connected. We're supposed to see Susan and Scott later this week for dinner. It's so wonderful we have family members to spend time with.

Andrew and I are sitting on the porch and chit-chatting when suddenly Billy's voice emerges from behind me. "Grandma?"

I spin around and see Billy standing there with his sleepy eyes and flailing arms.

"Oh, hi, little buddy." I stand up and go to scoop him up. He never resists. "How did you sleep, sweetheart?"

"Good." Billy is a boy of few words, but that's okay. We're still working on that.

"Are you hungry? I made you mac and cheese. Do you want that?"

"No." He shakes his head and rubs his eyes. He looks at me. "I want pizza."

"You want pizza?" I laugh.

Andrew grabs his phone right away. "I'm going to order us some pizza."

Andrew makes a killer grandfather. Everything Billy asks for, Billy gets instantly. I guess grandparents like to spoil their grandchildren, and we want him to have a better outlook on life, whatever has already been formed in his little head.

Billy is content on my lap, and he looks out somewhere in the distance while he's yawning.

"Grandma, can I have milk?"

"Of course you can have milk."

Andrew doesn't hesitate and goes to the kitchen right away to fulfill what he believes is his duty. I rock Billy gently and caress his hair and down his cheek. His face has become plumper in the past month, and he no longer looks malnourished.

"Park, Grandma?"

"You want to go to the park?"

"Yeah."

"We'll go to the park, sweetheart. Should we do it in the morning?"

Billy smiles. "Okay."

"And tomorrow afternoon. Tomorrow will be a special day."

"Why?" Billy asks. His whys have already begun.

"Why? It's because we're going to see your mommy."

"Mommy?"

"Yes. Your mommy. She wants to see you."

"See me?"

"Yes, love."

"I miss Mommy," Billy says.

I give him a gentle kiss on his cheek. "Me too, sweetheart. Me too."

CHAPTER 35

LUCY IS COMING to visit today.

Billy hasn't seen her since the CPS took him away. He has talked little about her; only once in a while when he goes to bed and wonders why his mom isn't there to tuck him in. Other than that, Billy has been content living with us. We've filled his days with many fun activities, distracting him from the trauma of his experiences. He's made progress with regulating his emotions better and not overreacting.

But for me—it's been over five years since I saw Lucy. Last time was in the courtroom. She was sitting in a pew with Fred, looking at me with stone-cold eyes and waiting for my verdict. The image of Lucy seems distorted in my mind. All I remember is that she looked like me when I was her age.

She has been in rehab and parent counseling for the past two-and-a-half months. We've received daily reports on her progress, and apparently, she has accepted that she needed to change drastically.

Lucy confessed that she'd been smoking so much weed she was helpless to care for Billy. There were nights she got so drunk, she'd pass out on the floor, oblivious to Billy's screams from across the house, begging for food.

It was all bad news. She wasn't fit to be a mother, and both she and Billy desperately needed help.

According to the report, a lot of grief and guilt went into her healing process. She has quit smoking weed and has chosen healthier life paths, such as daily workouts, good diet, and yoga.

We invited her over to our home for her first visit with Billy, as that was the best choice for him. Lucy and I have gone through so much turmoil in our relationship, and my heart flutters when I see her.

When she walks through the door, her eyes zoom in on Billy and she gasps at the first sight of him. She runs to him, kneels, and gives him a big hug, burying her face in his neck. Her body is convulsing; she must be crying.

Billy doesn't react. He just stands there, letting his mother sniff him like a dog who's just been reunited with his owner.

He finally puts his small arms around her neck and gives her a kiss.

Andrew and I exchange gazes and watch the display of deep affection unfold. I take more time to observe Lucy, who no longer looks like a young woman, barely crossed over from her teenage days. Everything about her has matured. I wonder if the change was sped up by all the time she'd spent learning to be a better parent the past few months. One can only hope.

She holds Billy for a couple of minutes, then pulls him away to look at his face. "My goodness, you're so grown." Her voice dominates love and pride. Her cheeks are flushed and covered in tears.

"Hi, Mommy," Billy says. He's awfully calm, and he seems to be okay in his mother's presence. "Where you been?"

"Ohhh." Lucy cracks. She's holding tears and can barely talk. She puts her knuckles on her mouth and watches him, pain etched in her eyes. "I've been away, baby. But I'm back. I am here for you now. Okay? I won't be going anywhere."

Lucy stands up and holds Billy's hand, before turning to me, daggers shooting from her eyes. "May we have a word?"

She sounds so formal. She must be angry with me for taking her child away. I don't blame her.

Once I discovered that Andrew's sister, Susan, was the daycare director, I teased information out of her about Lucy—where she lived, how she lived—and that's how I found out I had a grandson. Andrew went to Lucy's place to observe and record the dynamic between her and Billy, something that had already worried Susan. When I saw the footage of a drunken Lucy, nearly lifeless on the floor, with Billy tugging at her sleeve, trying to wake her up, my heart shattered into a million pieces. I had to do something, even if it was illegal. I had to take Billy away and save him.

I know the feeling of a child being taken away.

It's absolutely the worst feeling in the world.

But it had to happen.

People tend to appreciate things more when they are taken away from them. Like the way I appreciate my freedom after being jailed. Or Danny appreciating his mobility before he ended up in wheelchair. And it worked for Lucy. Because she would do anything to get her boy back.

"Sure." I nod.

"Privately." Her voice is stern.

I look at Andrew, and he shrugs, then gives a few quick nods, as if to give a nudge of encouragement.

Billy looks confused and gazes at his mom. "Mom will be right back," Lucy tells him. She kneels again and kisses him on his cheek.

Andrew approaches Billy and tells him he wants to show him something, to distract him.

"Follow me," I say.

We go to the den in the house's corner, and I try not to feel overwhelmed by the proverbial dark cloud hanging above us. I step inside the den and hold the door open to let Lucy in. She storms in with an angry energy, her eyes fixated in front of her. I close the door and offer her to sit down.

"It's alright," she says.

"Fine. How have you been, Lucy?" I inject empathy into my voice, but it doesn't fly with her.

"What do you care? Why did you take Billy away?" She raises her voice. "Why?"

"Calm down, Lucy. I promise we'll talk about Billy. I know how much he means to you. But there are a few other things I really need to discuss with you first."

"Like what?" If Lucy could stab me in the eye, I know she would.

I pause and wonder where to begin. I gaze down to gather my wits, then look at Lucy straight in the eye. "You knew Jimmy intended to kill me, didn't you? You knew it, yet you didn't want to say anything? You knew he messed with my brakes. You saw him, Lucy." I can hear the pain in my own voice.

Lucy's shoulders slump, and some of the anger seeps away from her. She scoffs, "Well, you killed him, and you said nothing about that. It's not like you weren't secretive. You knew I was looking for Jimmy. I was dying to see him."

She's got me there. I don't know what to say.

She goes for the verbal punch. "You killed your husband and hoped to get away with it."

I guess that's the jab I probably deserve. "You're right, Lucy. You're right. I've made so many mistakes, and you can blame me for that. But I've been working hard to improve myself. Five years in prison gives you a fresh perspective on life."

She scoffs. "I bet."

I squint my eyes at her. "What's that supposed to mean?"

She shakes her head. "Nothing."

But I think it's something.

"Speaking of prisons, how come you never told me anything about Evan?" I probe.

She widens her eyes, surprised to hear me question her about this. She shrugs. "It wasn't a big deal. He was just a buddy I hung out with."

"Right," I say. "It was a strange coincidence that we both knew him."

"Well, I can say for the first time that I agree."

I cock my head. "Wait, you didn't know I knew him?"

She slowly shakes her head. "No. I had no idea."

This's interesting. It just means life throws you a surprise when you don't expect it. Lucy and I had a close connection that we didn't even know about, and that's telling.

"Tell me why I should stick around," Lucy presses on.

"Do you not want to stick around? Do you just want to abandon this relationship completely?"

Her nostrils flare, and she looks like she wants to attack me. "Well, it doesn't take Einstein to realize I don't trust you, Lynn. You could have come clean, but you kept piling up those endless lies, pretending you were innocent."

I don't deny any of what Lucy says, and, for the first time, her words don't sting. "Our trust issues need to be revisited. I get it. But we can't improve it unless we work on it."

"Sure. And how do you suggest we work on it?"

"Therapy." I pause. "Listen, I'm your mother. I've made many mistakes, but at the end of the day, I love you and I want the best for you. Now you can understand being a parent isn't easy, but we do our best, right? And sometimes, no matter what we do, the child could resent us or be dissatisfied with us."

Her mind is churning, I can tell. She blinks a couple of times and looks like she wants to smile, but recoils.

"But we're both adults now, Lucy," I continue. "We can have a beautiful life together."

She's still not convinced. "I can't shake off our past. I don't know how to move on."

I nod, understanding. "Listen, Lucy. Whatever has happened, it's time to move on and give this relationship another chance. Because I cannot imagine my life without Billy in it."

Her eyes dart across me as if she's contemplating my words.

She nods. "Yes. I guess you're right. But it will take some time."

"Of course, honey." A tear escapes my eye. "All I want for us is to be happy. Together."

"I know." She nods.

"So, we will start all over again and take our time. We can start therapy soon and take our time. It can only get better from here. Rome wasn't built in a day."

Lucy looks at me in defeat. She studies me, and a smile slowly plasters itself across her face. "Billy and I definitely need you."

I nod. "Of course, and I'm here for you."

"Speaking of Rome," she says. "That could be our next trip." She chuckles softly.

"That sounds like a good plan. We can focus on fun times. Pinky promise?" I remember her telling me once Mary used to say "pinky promise" all the time and how much she loved it.

Lucy smiles. "Pinky promise."

She gives me a big hug. Her body convulses as the sobs overwhelm her. While a dark cloud hung above us for a while, our future now looks bright. There's still a lot of love to spread around.

Now I have everything in life, everything my heart has always desired. A loving partner, a beautiful daughter, a healthy grandson.

It's the people we love that make a happy life.

As Lucy and I walk back to the living room to hang out with the family for the afternoon, we hug each other and swap an occasional glance.

Then a thought occurs to me about how all this began. It was on that sunny day when I bought the lottery ticket that my life turned upside down. It was what changed everything for better or for worse, but ultimately for the better.

Would I dare buy another lottery ticket ever again? I chuckle to myself and think, never again!

. . .

--

Thank you for reading the Lottery series!
Please follow me on Amazon for new releases and check
out my other books.

ACKNOWLEDGMENTS

If you're reading this, you're the first person I need to thank for sticking with Lynn's story!

I'm so grateful for your support and for following Lynn's journey, even though I didn't initially plan this as a series. After publishing the first book, many readers felt that there were still unanswered questions, which inspired me to delve deeper and provide more satisfying conclusions.

After the second book, some readers felt that Lynn's ending—serving time in jail—was too harsh. This feedback motivated me to write a third and final book to redeem her. I sincerely hope that the conclusion in this final install-ment brings you the closure and satisfaction you've been waiting for.

A special thanks to my editor, Jess Ryn, who has been with me through every book in the series. Her keen eye and dedication have been invaluable in shaping Lynn's story. Without her, this journey would have been far more challenging.

I also want to extend my gratitude to a few readers who eagerly anticipated each new release: Alison, Anita, Brit-tany, Denise, Felecia, Mandy, Monica... Your enthusiasm and support have been incredibly motivating, and I deeply appreciate your support.

To the two most important people in my life—my husband and son—words cannot express how much I love you both. You make everything in life more beautiful.

Thank you all for being a part of this journey!

THANK YOU

I sincerely thank you for reading this book!

Please consider leaving a review, even if it's only a sentence, checking out my other books, and subscribing to my website. I'm also happy to answer any questions you may have, so do please get in touch with me via my website:

https://nadijamujagic.com

SUBSCRIBE

If you'd like to keep up to date with my latest releases, or get news about occasional free or discounted books, please sign up at the link below. We'll never share your email address and you can unsubscribe anytime:

https://nadijamujagic.com

ABOUT THE AUTHOR

Nadija Mujagić was born and raised in Sarajevo, Bosnia and Herzegovina, what used to be the former Yugoslavia back in the late 1970s. In 1997, she moved to the United States shortly after the end of the Bosnian War and has lived in Massachusetts since. In her spare time, she enjoys playing sports and electric bass guitar. *Lottery of Revenge* is her tenth book.